The Long Way Home

Family Tree

The Long Way Home

The Second Generation

ANN M. MARTIN

Scholastic Press / New York

Library of Congress Cataloging-in-Publication Data

Martin, Ann M., 1955– author.
The long way home / Ann M. Martin.
pages cm. — (Family tree ; book two)
Summary: Dana is Abby and Zander's daughter, but growing up in New York City in the late nineteen fifties is not always easy, especially when you would like your own room separate from your twin sister — and when your beloved father dies and you are forced to move things just get worse.
ISBN 978-0-545-35943-6 (jacketed hardcover) 1. Families — New York (State) — New York — Juvenile fiction. 2. Twins — Juvenile fiction. 3. Fathers and daughters — Juvenile fiction. 4. Mothers and daughters — Juvenile fiction. 5. New York (N.Y.) — History — 1951 — Juvenile fiction. [1. Family life — New York (State) — New York — Fiction. 2. Twins — Fiction. 3. Fathers and daughters — Fiction. 4. Mothers and daughters — Fiction. 5. New York (N.Y.) — History — 1951 — Fiction.] I. Title.
PZ7.M3567585Lq 2013
813.54 — dc23
2013018597

10 9 8 7 6 5 4 3 2   13 14 15 16 17

Printed in the U.S.A.   23
First edition, November 2013

The text type was set in Baskerville MT.
Book design by Elizabeth B. Parisi

For Adele Martin Vinsel,
my own Aunt Adele

Chapter 1

The smells drifting through the wide-open window of Dana Burley's bedroom weren't exactly pleasant, but they weren't exactly unpleasant either. She sniffed cautiously. Garbage truck, for sure. She had heard the grinding of gears and the rattle of metal cans and the calls of Howard and Arnold, who got to ride around all day long on the back of the truck, hanging on with just one hand and leaning merrily out into traffic. She sniffed again. She could smell exhaust, too, from the cars and taxis that rumbled along Eleventh Street, but mixed with everything else was the scent of leaves from the maple tree outside her window, and, drifting up from downstairs, various cooking smells — coffee and eggs and something sweet, which might be a birthday cake.

From across the room, as if she had read Dana's mind (and she probably had), Julia said, "I think I smell our birthday cake."

Dana pretended she was still asleep.

"Dana? I know you're awake."

This was one of the problems with having a twin sister. Dana had no secrets from her. Well, hardly any. She rolled over and looked across the room at Julia.

"We're seven today!" exclaimed Julia. "Aren't you excited?"

Dana grinned. "Yes."

"How come you didn't answer me before?"

Dana shrugged beneath her cotton blanket, then tossed it back. She sat up in bed and looked out the window just in time to see the garbage truck disappear from view, Howard waving to Mrs. Morgan, who was walking her poodle to the corner. Dana turned and surveyed the bedroom she shared with Julia. She thought of a word her art teacher had recently explained: *symmetry*. Her room certainly was symmetrical. You could see, on one side, Dana's domain, and on the other side, the reverse image, as if someone had held a mirror up to Dana's things. This was because every time Dana added something to her side, Julia hurried to add the same thing to the other side. If Dana asked her mother to look for a blue spread for her bed, Julia begged for the same blue spread. If Dana began a collection of marbles and arranged them in a tray on her bookcase, then — surprise, surprise — Julia suddenly became interested in marbles and arranged them on her bookcase on the opposite wall.

Even worse, most mornings, Julia waited until Dana had gotten dressed and then put on the exact same outfit.

"We're too old for samesies," Dana had said over and over again.

"But we're twins. *Identical* twins. We're special," Julia had replied.

"Mommy, she's copying me!" Dana would complain to their mother, and Abby would say patiently, "She looks up to you. She just wants to be like you, lovey. You should be flattered."

Dana was, after all, nine minutes older than Julia.

"Hi," came a husky voice from the doorway.

Dana patted her bed, and her brother ran across the room and dove onto her pillows. Then he sat placidly next to Dana, his eyes flat, his mouth hanging open slightly. "It's your birthday," he said seriously. Actually, what he said was, "It your birfday."

"That's right!" cried Julia, rolling out of her own bed and joining Dana and Peter. "You remembered. Do you know how old we are?"

"Five?" guessed Peter. His tongue protruded from his mouth and he breathed heavily.

"No, *you're* five," said Dana. She didn't want to hurt his feelings, though, so she added, "But that was a good guess."

"Party?" asked Peter.

"Yup, there's a party today, and a magician is —"

"Cake?" Peter interrupted.

"Yes, there will be cake," said Julia.

"I like cake," Peter announced.

"We know you do," said Dana. "Come on. Let's go downstairs. But first, do you need to use the potty?"

Peter didn't answer and Dana hurried into his room, pulled back the covers, and saw the wet stain on the sheets. Potty training was not going well.

"Do you need a diaper today?" asked Dana as she handed her brother a fresh pair of pajama bottoms.

Peter stepped into them and headed for the stairs. "I don't know."

Dana passed him. Then, followed by her sister and brother, she hurtled down the stairs to the second floor, ran by their parents' bedroom, and hurtled down another flight of stairs, jumping over the last two steps to make a dramatic entrance in the hallway.

"Are those the birthday girls?" their father called from the kitchen.

"Yes!" cried Dana and Julia, making their breathless way to the breakfast table.

"And me!" said Peter.

"And you," agreed Zander Burley, pulling Peter into his lap. He looked at the twins. "My goodness. Seven years old. What do you suppose is going to happen to you girls this year?"

Dana slid into her place at the table and watched her mother drop orange halves in the juicer and pump the arm up and down, juice flowing out the other side into a glass.

"Well," said Dana slowly, "I'm going to start second grade."

"*We're* going to start second grade," said Julia pointedly.

"And I'm going to keep taking art lessons with Mrs. Booth." Dana glanced at her sister. This was one claim that Julia couldn't make. She had no interest in art.

Abby turned away from the juicer and bent to kiss each of her children on the head. "Happy birthday," she said to Dana. "Happy birthday," she said to Julia. "Good morning, lovey," she said to Peter.

"Presents!" Peter shouted suddenly.

Dana's mother smiled. "Peter knows where your birthday presents are hidden."

"Ooh, can we open them now?" asked Julia. "Please?"

Dana stared out the window at the garden behind their town house.

"Don't you want to open our presents now?" Julia prodded her.

Dana hesitated. "I didn't ask for anything."

"Well, you know you're getting presents anyhow," said Julia.

Dana continued to study the garden.

Her father eyed her from across the table. "Is there something you haven't told us?"

Dana picked up her spoon and saw her warped reflection in it. "There is one thing I want, but it isn't something you can buy."

Now everyone was staring at her.

"I get the presents?" said Peter, heading for the door.

No one answered him.

"Dana? Lovey?" said her mother.

"I want my own room," Dana whispered.

Julia opened her mouth and then closed it again.

"Please?" said Dana. "I know you think Julia and I want to share a room."

"We do!" exclaimed Julia. "We do!"

"*You* do. But I don't. I don't want everything to be samesies. I want to be just myself in my own room. We could turn the den into my room. Please?" Dana said again. "It's right next to our bedroom, Julia, so we'd be next door to each other."

"No!"

"We already have a library downstairs, and, Daddy, you have your study on the top floor, so it isn't like we *need* a den. It could be my room, my very own room."

Dana saw her parents exchange a glance over her head. She had long ago realized that Abby and Zander could talk to each other with just their eyes. That was how close they were. They had known each other since grade school, which was a long time. True, they had become separated when Zander had gone off to fight in World War II, but after he had come home, he'd tracked Abby down in New York City and proposed to her (for the second time). Now they had been together for ten years, and seemed, to Dana, to live secret, impenetrable lives.

"This is something Daddy and I need to discuss, lovey," Abby said to Dana. "We're not saying no. We just need to talk about it."

"And we might not have a chance to talk about it today," said Zander. "Too much going on. We have party preparations this morning —"

"Cake!" cried Peter, who had returned, presentless, to the table.

"Yes, cake," his father repeated fondly. "And then there's the party this afternoon and your special evening tonight."

Dana's thoughts, ever since she had begun to eye the den as her future bedroom, had not been on her birthday, but now she began to feel excited. "Pockets the Clown will be here, Peter! Remember Pockets? He came to your fourth birthday party." She turned to her parents. "Thank you," she said. To Julia she added, "You'll have your own room, too, you know. Won't that be great? You can have privacy and —"

"I just want you," muttered her sister.

"Now I get the presents?" said Peter, heading for the door again. And when he returned with an armload of wrapped packages, Julia brightened. She said no more about Dana's birthday wish.

Dana's mother had worried that the day would be rainy or that a thunderstorm would come along in the afternoon. She wanted to be able to hold the party in the garden, although Dana didn't see why they couldn't have the party indoors, since their town house was enormous. But the sun shone all day long, and Dana and her family and the twelve guests were entertained in the bright, humid July air of a New York afternoon by Pockets the Clown and Sinbad the Magician.

Peter wore a suit and tie and his new brown oxfords, and Dana and Julia wore party dresses that stood out stiffly with crinoline. (Julia had waited to see which dress Dana would wear and had selected the matching one, and then Dana had secretly changed into a different party dress when it was too late for Julia to do anything about it.)

In the garden Dana sat surrounded by her four best friends, holding hands with her two *best* best friends, until Julia unhitched Marian Hackenburg's hand from Dana's and replaced it with her own. The guests watched, fascinated, as Pockets pulled twenty-five American flags from a pocket the size of a postage stamp, and then pulled fifteen gumdrops from an equally small pocket and passed them out to the children. Later they watched Sinbad turn a bottle of milk into a dove, and make a rose disappear . . . only to turn up later in Peter's ear. This came as no surprise to Peter, who simply smiled vaguely. Dana realized that this was because Peter didn't understand enough to know that a rose shouldn't be in his ear in the first place, but everyone else was amazed and clapped loudly for Sinbad when the show was over.

Later there was ice cream and cake, and before the twins opened the presents from their friends, they all took turns whacking a stick at a donkey-shaped piñata that Dana's father had hung from a limb of the gingko tree. Marian was the one whose crashing blow finally broke the piñata open, and then everyone scrambled to gather up the candies and trinkets. Patty Morris gave all of her candy to Peter.

The party ended, the guests went home, and Dana was in the garden examining her presents — pleased that several of her friends had chosen not to get identical gifts for her and Julia — when her mother called from the back door, "Girls, time to get ready for tonight. I think you'll both need baths before you put on fresh clothes."

Peter's babysitter arrived at five thirty.

"Can't Peter come with us, Daddy?" asked Dana.

"He isn't quite old enough for *Plain and Fancy*," said her father. "He'd get too wiggly. Remember how wiggly he was the last time we went to the theatre? We'll do something fun together on the weekend."

"How about tomorrow?"

"Tomorrow is Friday. I already took one day off from writing. I need to get back to work. The book is due in a month. Now go change! Our chariot awaits."

The chariot was not a chariot and it wasn't waiting. It was a cab the Burleys caught at the corner of Eleventh Street and Sixth Avenue, and it drove them to the 21 Club for a very grown-up dinner before they walked to the Winter Garden Theatre, where *Plain and Fancy* was playing.

"This certainly is different from the birthdays I used to have," said Dana's mother as they settled into their seats in the theatre.

"You didn't go to any musicals?" asked Julia.

"Your daddy and I lived in a very small town in Maine. There was only one theatre and it was a movie theatre. And when I was little, we hardly had any money. I didn't even have a birthday party until I was eleven. Then we had a picnic on the beach. I thought it was very grand."

"A picnic? That was all?" said Dana.

"Well, it was a very nice picnic and lots of people came. And your aunt Rose and I got new dresses."

"Were you there, Daddy?"

"I was. But I hardly knew your mother then. I already liked her, though," he said, and reached across Dana's lap to take Abby's hand.

"Don't kiss her!" Dana hissed, and Julia giggled. "Not in public!"

The lights dimmed then, the orchestra began to play, and Dana settled in her seat, her eyes on the stage as the curtain rose.

She felt quite grown-up, having eaten dinner at the 21 Club, and sitting now in the Winter Garden, surrounded by dressed-up theatergoers, mostly adults. She had a feeling that this year was going to be very different from any year before.

Chapter 2

The best thing about catching the flu (and there actually had been several good things about it) was that during the long days her mother had confined Dana to bed, Dana had made a vast number of Christmas decorations for her room. Looped over her window was a string of gold and silver stars, and in the center of each, Dana had drawn a different illustration from "The Twelve Days of Christmas" — a French hen (even though she had no idea what a French hen was), a leaping lord, a milkmaid — trying to remember everything she'd learned from Mrs. Booth, her art teacher. Taped to her closet door was a paper tree, and dangling from its boughs were individual paper ornaments. At the top of the tree was an angel with yellow yarn for her hair and tiny brown buttons for her eyes. And draped everywhere — swooping from the ceiling, trailing from bedpost to bedpost, connecting lamp to bookshelf to doorknob — were green-and-red paper chains, the links held together with goopy paste, just like the paste Dana and Julia used in their second-grade room at Miss Fine's School.

Now the flu was gone, although Dana was still coughing (so were Julia and Peter), but the wondrous decorations remained. And, Dana noted with some satisfaction, Julia hadn't even begun to try to make similar ones for her room. The days of samesies were fading.

Dana glanced out the window of her new bedroom, saw snowflakes falling lightly onto the softened world of Eleventh Street, and tiptoed into the hallway. The doors to Julia's and Peter's rooms were still closed, but from the first floor came low voices. Dana started down the stairs, reached the second floor, and listened again. Her mother's voice was raised slightly; her father's sounded tired, as if he had been explaining something over and over again. Or maybe defending himself.

"Could you just please confine it to the evening after the children have gone to bed?" said her mother sharply.

"Don't make rules for me, Abigail," her father replied.

Dana's mother said something else, which Dana couldn't catch, and then her father said, "I didn't think it was so important."

"Well, it is. It's —"

Her mother stopped speaking as Dana suddenly ran full tilt down the last flight of stairs and burst into the kitchen. "Good morning!" she said brightly.

Her parents looked up from their coffee. In the lull that followed, Dana became aware that the radio was on and caught the words *Rosa Parks* and then the words *bus boycott.*

"Rosa Parks did a very courageous thing," her father said into the awkward atmosphere of the kitchen.

Dana nodded. "She's the Negro lady who refused to give up her seat on the bus just so a white person could sit down instead," she said, pleased with her knowledge. "But then they made her pay a fine!" she added indignantly. "That wasn't right."

"It certainly wasn't," agreed her mother.

Dana's parents loosened their grips on their coffee cups. They looked at each other and held one of their eye conversations. Even Dana could understand this one. Their argument, whatever it had been about, would be continued later, in private.

"It's important to stand up for what you believe in," said Abby.

"And to think of the other person," said Zander. "Apparently, the white people on the bus didn't stop to think that Rosa Parks might need to sit down after a long day at work."

"Always be nice," added Dana.

She thought of the little boy who had laughed and pointed at Peter in the grocery store the day before and wondered if Peter remembered this. With Peter, it was hard to tell.

Dana's mother switched off the radio and opened the Frigidaire. "Breakfast time," she announced.

And Dana said, "Daddy, can we get the Christmas decorations out today?"

The decorations were kept in large cardboard boxes stored in the closet shaped like a triangle underneath the staircase to the third floor. For eleven months out of every year, the boxes sat in the dark in forlorn, musty stacks. Sometimes Dana peeked in at them on a sweltering summer day, just to see how they were doing. But early each December, her father hauled the boxes out and carried them to the first floor. This was one of Dana's favorite days of the year, almost as good as Christmas Day itself.

That morning, the snow still falling, Dana and Julia and Peter opened carton after carton and exclaimed over all the things they hadn't seen since the previous January, when the decorations had been put away.

"Here's the Santa Claus music box!" cried Julia.

"Look! Look! Dolly!" said Peter, holding up the fragile angel that had once belonged to Zander's mother.

"When can we get our tree?" asked Dana.

"Tomorrow," said her father. "We'll put out the other decorations now and get the tree tomorrow."

"Then I'm going to make ornaments today! And I'm going to ask Marian and Patty to come over. Can I, Daddy? Please? We have paper and glitter and crayons and sequins. We can make all sorts of things."

Julia slumped into a chair. "Why do you have to ask Marian and Patty? *I'll* make ornaments with you."

"All four of us can make ornaments. Peter, too, if he wants. It will be fun."

"It would be more fun if it was just for twins," said Julia, but Dana was already heading for the telephone table in the front hall.

An hour later Marian and Patty arrived, stomping the snow off their boots as they waved good-bye to their mothers.

"We have the whole kitchen table for our workshop!" Dana said, and soon she and Julia and their friends were busily snipping and gluing. Peter stood at one end of the table and watched.

"Don't you want to make something?" Marian asked him.

Peter rocked from side to side. "Goo," he said.

"Yes, glue," agreed Dana. Then she reminded him, "Glue is for gluing, not for eating."

Peter wandered away and the girls returned to their paper ornaments. Dana's were complicated affairs — folded creations with illustrations on them, or sometimes hidden inside. When a small stack had piled up in the center of the table, Julia said, "I'm tired of making decorations."

"Me, too, but I have an idea. Let's make a mural now," said Dana. "A Christmas mural. We can all work on it at the same time. We'll each do different parts. We're learning about murals in art class," she added, turning to Julia, who was the only one of the girls not taking art lessons from Mrs. Booth.

"A mural? But I can't draw."

Marian was already searching through the crayons. "I'm going to make Santa coming down the chimney!" she exclaimed.

"I'm going to make the manger scene," said Patty.

Dana found a length of butcher paper. The mural was half finished before she realized that Julia had left the kitchen.

*　　*　　*

The snow fell all day long. After Marian and Patty left, Patty carrying not only her ornaments but the mural, since the girls had decided to share it and had drawn straws to see who would get to keep it first, Dana stood in the kitchen and looked at her tin box full of Crayola crayons. Outside it was dark, but the kitchen and the crayons were bright, and Dana liked the contrast. It had been a very good, Christmasy day so far.

Her father stuck his head around the corner. "How did the ornament making go?"

Dana pointed to her creations. "We made a mural, too. Patty is keeping it first."

Zander examined the ornaments. "Beautiful," he said finally. "You're very talented, honey."

"Thank you."

"Your mother and I had an idea. How about if we go uptown and look at the tree at Rockefeller Center and then have ice cream at Rumpelmayer's?"

"Really? Right now?"

"Right now. Hurry and get ready. Our chariot awaits."

The taxi ride to Rockefeller Center was slow and slippery and exciting. Every time the cab slid unstoppably sideways, the driver muttering and pumping the brakes, Peter cried, "Whoo! Whoo!" and sometimes, "Again!"

Dana's mother put her hands over her eyes, and her father gripped the strap by the window with one hand and Peter with the other. But when they finally stepped out onto Fifth Avenue, Zander gave the man a large tip and said, "Merry Christmas to you."

The tree was dazzling. Dana remembered the year before, when she and Julia had watched the lighting of the tree on *The Howdy Doody Show*. But they hadn't seen the tree in person. Now she stood with her back to Fifth Avenue, facing the grandeur of Rockefeller Center, and gazed at the magnificent tree, which was rising up beyond the skating rink, awash in tiny lights.

"My tree?" said Peter from his father's arms.

Zander laughed. "No, this isn't your tree. Ours will be a lot smaller."

"Can we come here every year and see the tree?" asked Julia.

"I think we should make it a Burley family tradition," said Abby.

Later, sitting in Rumpelmayer's, her favorite restaurant in the world, and sipping a milkshake through two straws, Dana decided that even if Christmas never arrived, this day — this moment with her family — would be just as good.

*   *   *

Dana's father waited until the twins and Peter had their baths and were in their pajamas before he opened the liquor cabinet in the library and poured his first drink of the evening. By the time Dana was ready to say good night to him, his words sounded mushy, and now he had tripped over Peter's teddy bear and landed on the floor of the library on his bottom, where he sat laughing.

"Daddy?" said Dana.

"Go on to bed," said her mother from behind her. "Right now."

Dana turned and started for the stairs. She could hear her mother say sharply, "Get up." And "I asked you to wait until the children were asleep, at the very least."

Dana paused. "He was *laughing*," she told her mother. "He wasn't —"

"Bed, Dana. Right this instant."

"Good night, Daddy. I love you," Dana called over her shoulder.

"I'll be up in a minute," said her mother.

Dana didn't answer. She stomped to her room and turned off the light. Later, when Abby poked her head around the door, Dana lay still, her face toward the wall. Abby sighed and closed the door softly. After a long time Dana flicked on the lamp beside her bed, tiptoed to her closet, and retrieved a box that she'd hidden at the back. On the top she had written Merry Christmas to Daddy and Mommy. She sat on the floor, opened the box, and looked through the drawings she'd been working on with Mrs. Booth — sketches of everyone in her family, plus one of their house and another of the view of Eleventh Street from the window in the living room.

She replaced the top on the box, thought for a moment, then found an eraser and slowly rubbed out the words *and Mommy*.

Chapter 3

Wednesday, July 18th, 1956

"Can you believe that Mommy and Aunt Rose used to wake up in this bed every single morning?" said Julia, rubbing her eyes. She slithered from under the covers, rested her arms on the windowsill, and looked down at Blue Harbor Lane as she breathed in the damp, salty air. "I wonder what Mommy saw when she looked out this window."

"The same view you see, silly," said Dana sleepily.

"I don't mean just the view. Mommy would see people outside, people who don't live here in Lewisport any-more. Or maybe she had a dog, and the dog sat in the front yard and barked at cars. I wonder what cars looked like back then."

Dana yawned. "Mom said that when she used to live here, there weren't even screens on the windows. Think of all the bugs that must have flown inside when the windows were open."

"Think of a whole family crammed into this teeny space," said Julia. "Mommy and Aunt Rose didn't even have their own *beds*."

"Think of living here with Papa Luther," said Dana.

"Think of living anywhere with Papa Luther. He's scary."

"We have to visit him today."

"But just for a minute," said Julia. "And not until later. Come on. Mommy said we were going to take a walk on the beach this morning."

Dana, now fully awake, scrambled out of bed and followed Julia down the stairs of the little beach house in Maine. She found her mother and Peter sitting on the front stoop, looking across the street at the ocean.

"Crash!" announced Peter. "Waves crash! I swim?"

"Yes, we'll go swimming today," said his mother.

"Where's Dad?" asked Dana.

"Still asleep."

"Not anymore." Dana's father, looking rumpled, joined his family on the stoop. "It's a treat to be so leisurely," he said. "Let's sleep late every morning of our vacation."

"Shall we take our walk?" asked Dana's mother.

"In pajamas?" asked Peter.

"No!" Abby laughed. "Everybody, go change. We'll take a walk and then we'll have breakfast."

Ten minutes later Dana and her family set off in the wet sand. Peter lagged behind with Zander, stopping frequently to examine shells or to sift sand through his fingers, while Abby and the girls marched briskly ahead.

"The water's freezing!" cried Julia.

"It doesn't ever get very warm," replied her mother. "Not up here in Maine."

"How long did you live in Lewisport?" Julia wanted to know.

"Until I was ten. I had just turned ten when we moved to the big house in Barnegat Point."

"And who were your friends when you lived here?" Dana asked. She already knew the answer to this question. She and Julia asked their mother the same questions every time they visited the beach house in Maine. They liked hearing her answers.

"Well, I suppose Rose was my best friend, but I didn't know it. Back then she was just my little sister. My best friend who was my own age was Sarah."

"The one who drowned," said Julia.

"Yes, the one who drowned. And then there was Orrin."

"The boy your father didn't like," said Dana. She stooped to examine a clam shell, rinsed the sand off it in a whoosh of seawater, and stuck it in the pocket of her shorts.

"What about Daddy?" asked Julia.

"I didn't meet your daddy until we moved."

"And what did you and Rose and Sarah and Orrin used to do together?"

"We picked blueberries and went clamming. And Sarah and I made paper dolls and skipped rope and read mystery stories."

"Did you ever go to New York City?" asked Dana.

"Never. Not until I was a grown-up. New York seemed like a faraway country."

The Burleys walked along until Julia said her feet were turning to ice, and then they returned to the cottage for breakfast.

After breakfast they climbed into the car that Papa Luther, Abby's father, had lent them. The Burleys didn't own a car — they didn't need one in New York — and Dana was always fascinated to watch her father behind the wheel. "Drive like a cabbie!" she called from the backseat, and Zander laughed.

"Not on your life," he said as he steered the car slowly down Blue Harbor Lane and turned onto the road to Barnegat Point.

The Burleys rode through town and then out of town and then along a bumpy street with only a handful of houses on it, set so far back that Dana couldn't get a good look at them. Her sketch pad was in her lap and she wanted to see the houses, but settled on studying the birds and trees they passed, and the little lanes leading back to the ocean, brilliant in the morning sun and glitter of white sand.

"Here we are," Dana's mother said presently.

"Aunt Rose?" asked Peter.

"That's right. This is Aunt Rose's house."

The house, much bigger than the beach cottage, but not nearly as big as the enormous house in Barnegat Point that Dana's mother had moved to when she was ten, looked friendly to Dana. She thought so every single time she saw it. The wood shingles were fading in a pleasant manner, and gingham curtains, handmade by Rose, hung in each window.

Before the Burleys had even stepped out of the car, the front door of the house opened and out bounded Dana's cousins, followed by her aunt Rose and her uncle Harry.

"We got a badminton set!" announced Emily, who was seven.

"And we're all going to play," added William, who was five.

"Except I'm too short," said Lizzie, who was three.

"Come around back," added Teddy, the oldest cousin. He was so much older than the other cousins that he was already a teenager. Thirteen years old, an age Dana aspired to be. She was slightly jealous of Teddy, just because of his age.

"I play?" Peter wanted to know.

"We'll teach you," said Teddy.

Dana and Julia and the cousins did try very patiently to teach Peter to play badminton. But he couldn't hit the birdie and eventually he threw his racket on the ground and screeched.

"Peter," said Lizzie, "don't cry. I can't hit that bird either."

"It's a birdie," said Emily.

"I don't care," said Lizzie.

"Mean game!" shouted Peter.

"What's going on out there?" an adult voice called through an open window at the back of the house.

"Is it lunchtime yet?" asked Dana.

Luckily it was.

Peter sputtered and cried and kicked at stones on his way to the house, but when he found that lunch was to be a picnic at the beach, a real picnic on a blanket in the sand, he brightened. "Central Park!" he announced.

"What?" said William.

"We had a picnic in Central Park last week," Dana told her cousin. "That's a big park in New York City."

"I wish I could go to New York," said Emily.

"So do I," said Aunt Rose. She knelt on the picnic blanket and handed plates around.

Dana studied her aunt, who wore her hair wound up on her head, a blue-flowered blouse that she had made herself, and a look of longing for all the things Dana saw every day in New York. "You should visit us sometime," said Dana. "All of you. Uncle Harry, have you ever been to New York?"

"Nope."

Aunt Rose let out a small laugh. "I guess I don't *really* want to go anyway. I'm not a city girl. It's nice to dream about New York, that's all."

Uncle Harry, who never said much ("He's a man of few words," Dana's father liked to say), smiled and rubbed the spot between Aunt Rose's shoulder blades, the spot that always hurt at the end of a day's work.

The visit was over too soon, with Dana and her family climbing back into their borrowed car, and Aunt Rose and Dana's mother hugging each other through the open window.

"Why are we crying?" said Abby, wiping away tears. "We're going to see each other again tomorrow."

Aunt Rose fanned the air in front of her face, Uncle Harry put his arm around her, and soon the car was headed back to Barnegat Point.

"Do we *have* to visit Papa Luther and Helen?" asked Julia as the car neared the big house on Haddon Road. A whine had crept into her voice.

"Yes," replied Abby. "And no whining."

"I don't like Papa Lufer," said Peter from the backseat.

"I know, lovey," replied Abby. "But he's my father. He's part of our family."

The visit was wonderfully short. The Burleys stood uneasily on Papa Luther's front porch after Abby rang the bell.

"Aren't they expecting us?" asked Dana, recalling the enthusiastic greeting they'd gotten at Aunt Rose's house.

"Shh," said Abby. She swatted at Dana from behind her back.

Presently the door was opened by a maid who Dana didn't recall meeting the last time her family had visited Maine. She ushered the Burleys inside and soon Papa Luther and his wife, who was not Dana's grandmother, met them in the hallway and kissed them on their cheeks — everyone except Peter, for whom, Dana soon realized, Helen had set out "a special chair."

"It's just his size," she said as she led the way into the parlor.

Dana noticed that the chair was positioned far from the couch where Helen and Papa Luther sat. Peter looked very alone in it.

Dana's mother ended the visit quickly, even before Miles, who was Helen and Papa Luther's son, showed up. She scooped Peter into her arms and carried him outside, and the moment the door had closed behind them, she muttered, "Well, that's over with."

Dana let out her breath and took her father's hand.

"Let's walk into town," said Abby, setting Peter down.

"Daddy, that's where *you* grew up in, isn't it?" asked Julia, indicating the house next to Papa Luther's.

Zander nodded. "Yup. My bedroom was right up there." He pointed to a window on the side of the house.

"And why did your parents move?" asked Dana, who had never gotten a satisfying answer to the question.

"It was just time," her father replied.

Dana and her family spent the next hour walking through Barnegat Point, Abby and Zander stopping frequently to say, "There's where we went to school," or "See that movie theatre? It was the only one in town for years," or "That used to be a toy store."

"All right. Time to get our car and go back to the cottage," said Zander at last.

"Can't we stay in town just a little longer?" asked Julia.

"Nope," replied her mother. "Did you forget? Aunt Adele is coming for dinner tonight."

By the time Adele Nichols arrived at the beach cottage, Dana and Julia had made a WELCOME sign for her, which they'd strung above the front door. Dana thought her aunt Adele might be her favorite person in the world, apart from her parents and her brother and sister. She loved Aunt Rose and Uncle Harry and her cousins, and all of the Burley relatives, too. But Aunt Adele was special. She was young, much younger than Dana's parents, and she sat on the floor and played games with Dana and Julia and Peter, listened closely to whatever they had to say, hugged Peter, and laughed at her own jokes with her head thrown back. She still lived at home with Papa Luther and Helen, even though she was twenty-one years old. Papa Luther said she couldn't leave until she got married, but Aunt Adele wasn't interested in getting married. To make matters worse, Papa Luther wouldn't let her do any kind of work either, except help Mrs. Cabot, the seamstress in town.

Aunt Adele was stuck. That's what she told the Burleys at dinner that night.

"Unstick yourself," Dana suggested.

Her aunt looked at her seriously. "You know, that is very good advice."

When Dana finally fell into bed that night, she lay awake for a long time while Julia snored softly beside her. Apart from the visit to Papa Luther's house, the day had been perfect. An early walk on the beach, cousins, a picnic, a trip to Barnegat Point, and dinner with Aunt Adele. And her father hadn't touched a drop of alcohol.

Chapter 4

Sunday, October 21st, 1956

"Let's go wait outside," said Dana to her brother and sister. "Mom, can we wait for Aunt Adele outside?"

Dana's mother stepped out of the kitchen, wiping her hands on a dish towel. "All right. But keep Peter close by you. Don't go far."

"We'll stay on the stoop!" Dana called, and she and Julia and Peter opened the front door of their town house to a warm but windy October afternoon. They sat in a row on the top step and craned their necks to the left, straining for the first glimpse of their aunt as she walked along Eleventh Street from the subway.

Dana still could not believe that Aunt Adele actually lived in New York City now. Just three months had passed since Dana had suggested that her aunt unstick herself. A month after that, Adele announced to Papa Luther and Helen that she'd given notice to Mrs. Cabot, the seamstress, and that she had saved enough money to buy a train ticket to New York

City. There hadn't been much that Papa Luther could say to this. He knew that Dana's family would let Adele stay with them for as long as she liked. She had a train ticket and a place to live while she looked for work, and that was all she needed in order to leave Barnegat Point.

Two days later, Adele, carrying a large suitcase containing all of her clothes, had stepped off a train at Grand Central Station, where she was greeted by Abby, Dana, Julia, and Peter. She'd lived with the Burleys for a mere two weeks before she'd found what she considered her dream job — in Bobbie Palombo's costume shop.

"A costume shop?" Dana had said when Adele had rushed through the door of the town house with her good news.

This day also happened to be the first day of third grade for Dana and Julia, and the twins and their aunt had arrived home just minutes apart. "Our teacher is awful!" Julia was exclaiming to their mother and Peter, when Adele blew through the door.

"I found work!" Adele had cried. "Better than that, I found a job. A job I'm going to love."

"That's wonderful," Dana's mother had said. "What's the job?"

"I'll be working in a costume shop."

This was when Dana had said, "A costume shop?"

"It's owned by a woman named Bobbie Palombo, and the company designs costumes for films and Broadway shows," Adele had replied proudly. "At first I'll just be making the costumes, but maybe one day I'll design them, too. I'll get a paycheck in two weeks and then I'll start looking for my own apartment."

"Aren't you going to live here?" Dana had asked, dismayed.

"Not forever, sweetie. I love living here, but I want my own place. And you don't want me cluttering up your guest room forever."

"Yes, we do," Dana and Julia had insisted.

"Stay!" Peter had commanded.

But in no time, Aunt Adele had found an apartment on West Fifty-Third Street and had packed up her belongings. The apartment wasn't as close to Bobbie Palombo's as she would have liked, but it wasn't too far away either, and it was near the theatre district, so that when Adele was a bit more established, she could just walk to a Broadway show whenever she felt like it.

By the October Sunday when Dana sat expectantly on her front stoop with her brother and sister, she had visited Adele's apartment several times. It consisted of a small living room with a kitchen at one end, an even smaller bedroom, and the teensiest bathroom Dana had ever seen. The bathroom was so small that it didn't even have a tub in it, just a shower. Dana could stand in the middle of the bathroom and, turning in a circle with her arms outstretched, brush all four walls with her hands as she went around. Her aunt painted the walls of the living room pink and aqua, and she bought a red lamp shade that rattled with beads, and she set a birdcage on a pole by the window and grew an African violet in the cage. Dana thought the apartment was wonderful.

Peter was the first to spot Adele that afternoon. He shot to his feet. "Adele! I see her! Adele!"

Dana and Julia clattered down the steps, Peter at their heels, and they ran along Eleventh Street, stopping several feet from their aunt, when Julia said, "What's that?"

Adele was cradling something in her hands, something squirmy.

"A kitten," she replied. "I just found him. And I don't think he wants to be held."

"You just found him? Where?" asked Julia.

"In front of the sandwich shop on Sixth Avenue. He looks half starved. No one in the shop knew anything about him."

"Are you going to keep him?" Dana wanted to know. They were walking slowly back to the town house now, the kitten wiggling mightily.

Adele shook her head. "No pets allowed in my building."

"I keep him," said Peter firmly. He reached up to pat the kitten.

"We have to ask Mom and Dad first," Dana told him.

"Mommy!" yelled Peter the moment they stepped inside. "Mommy!"

"Peter, what is it? My goodness." Abby hurried out of the kitchen again, this time wiping her hands on her apron.

Adele, looking sheepish, held the kitten out to her sister. "I found him down the block. I didn't mean —"

"Can we keep him?" Dana interrupted her. "Adele isn't allowed to have pets at her apartment."

"Please?" said Julia.

"Please?" said Peter.

Adele placed the kitten in Peter's arms, and the wiggling and squirming came to an end. "He likes me," Peter announced. "Mine." He stroked the orange fur and presently they could all hear the kitten begin to purr.

"We have to talk to Daddy," said Dana's mother. "We have to make a family decision."

"Mine," said Peter again, settling cross-legged on the floor with the kitten in his lap.

"Family decision," Abby repeated. "Daddy will be home in an hour."

"His name is Tail," Peter continued. "Tail Burley."

Zander Burley's study was on the top floor of the town house. He wrote his novels there and answered his mail and made phone calls to his editor and agent. Dana heard the typewriter clacking away at all hours of the day and sometimes the night, too, weekdays, weekends, whenever her father said inspiration had struck. Dana hadn't read any of her father's books. They were too long and had too many big words, and anyway they were for grown-ups and didn't interest her. But they interested lots of other people. They were best sellers and they won awards and Zander was one of the most famous New York City writers of his time.

On the day when Adele arrived with Tail in her hands, Dana's father wasn't at home.

"I'm stuck," he had said that morning, which meant something very different from what Adele had meant when she'd said she was stuck. When Zander Burley was stuck, his words wouldn't come and he couldn't finish whatever scene or a chapter he was working on. Dana's mother called it writer's block and reminded her husband that it never lasted long. Zander said he didn't care what it was called or how long it lasted; it was still an awful feeling.

"So I need a change of scenery," he had continued. "Then I can finish this chapter." Not much later he had left the house, saying he'd be back in time for dinner with Adele.

Dana noted that he'd left the house empty-handed.

"Where's his work?" she'd asked her mother. "How is he going to write without all his papers?"

Her mother had shaken her head and disappeared, tight-lipped, up the stairs.

Which was how Dana knew her father was not going to finish his chapter, but instead was going to look up a few friends, and then they would all find some liquor together. The fact that it was Sunday didn't matter. Zander could find a drink anywhere at any time.

Dana's father came home just before dinner, as he had promised. By then Tail had pooped under the dining room table and also had climbed the living room curtains to such a height that Adele had needed to stand on a stepladder in order to unhook his claws from the fabric and hand him down to Peter.

"Huh," said Dana's mother, scrubbing the dining room rug with disinfectant. "If we're going to keep Tail, we'll need to remember to let him outside from time to time. And," she added, suddenly looking stern, "if Daddy agrees that we can keep Tail, someone is going to have to clean the poop out of the garden every day."

"We will! We will!" Julia and Dana cried.

"And we'll have to get a kitty bowl," Abby continued.

"A kitty bowl?" said a deep voice. Dana turned around to find that her father had returned and was standing in the front hall, looking from the stepladder by the living room window to the stain on the carpet. "What'sh going on?" he added, placing a steadying hand on the telephone table.

"Daddy!" Peter yelped. He held Tail aloft. "Look! I have a kitty."

"I found him this afternoon," said Adele hurriedly. "And the children want to keep him."

"But I said we have to make a family decision," added Abby. She paused. "If you're capable of making a decision."

"Of coursh I can make a deshision. Why couldn't I make a deshision?" (Dana's mother glared at him.) "What are we deshiding? Whether to keep the little kitty cat? Let ush keep it. Why not?"

"I'm not sure you're thinking clearly just now. We'll need to find a vet. And he's already pooped under —"

"It'sh one little tiny kitty cat. Go ahead and keep it."

"We can keep him! Daddy said!" exclaimed Julia, and Peter hugged Tail to his chest.

"I would hardly call this a discussion," muttered Dana's mother.

Dana's father took a step away from the table and stumbled into the wall. "Dinner ready?" he asked. "I am one hungry pershon, yup, one hungry pershon."

Dana saw Adele glance at Abby. "Are you sure you want me to stay?" Adele whispered. And then, "I'm sorry about the cat. I didn't mean to cause any trouble."

"Stay," said Abby. "It's all right."

The meal that followed was fight-free, although no one said much except Peter, who commented endlessly on Tail and what he was doing under the table, which, thankfully, did not include pooping.

By the time Abby was serving coffee, Dana's father looked less glassy-eyed. He smiled at Adele. "Tail has made Peter awfully happy," he remarked. "Thank you for finding him."

Adele left soon after, Julia and Peter took Tail upstairs to show him the bedrooms, and Dana sat in the library with her sketchbook.

"Productive day, dear?" she heard her mother say to her father in the living room:

"It got away from me. I met Frank and he knew about this bistro —"

"Why do you do it?"

Silence.

"Really, why do you do it?"

"Don't give me a hard time, Abby. I have a whopping headache."

"I'm not surprised."

Dana wanted to call, "Leave him alone! He let us keep Tail!" Instead she tucked her sketch pad under one arm, put her hands over her ears, and crept up the stairs to her room.

Chapter 5

Monday, June 3rd, 1957

"Dana! Over here!"

Dana, arms linked with Patty and Marian so they formed a chain at the top of the school steps, scanned the group of parents waiting on the sidewalk below.

"Dana!" the voice called again. Then, "Julia!"

"Adele!" Dana dropped Patty's and Marian's arms and ran down the steps to the edge of the little crowd, where Adele stood with Peter. "What are you doing here?" She threw her arms around her aunt.

"I have the afternoon off," she replied, and hugged Julia, who had joined them. "I told your mom I'd take you to the park."

"Goody!" cried Dana. "Can Patty and Marian come with us?"

"Patty and Marian?" said Julia, her face collapsing, just as Adele said, "Of course they can. Where are their mothers?"

Dana pointed. "Over there."

The grown-ups held a hurried conversation, and soon Dana, Julia, Peter, Marian, and Patty were walking lazily along Ninth Street with Adele.

"No homework, girls?" Adele asked.

Dana held out her empty hands. "Nope. None. School's almost over. Only one more week. Then no more third grade."

"School's out, school's out, teacher wore her bloomers out!" sang Marian.

"Bloomers!" Peter cried, and erupted in giggles.

They reached Sixth Avenue and turned right.

"I love this bakery," Adele said presently, pausing to look at an enormous wedding cake in a window display. "If I had a wedding cake, I wouldn't put a bride and groom on the top, though. I'd want the moon and a circle of stars instead."

"I'd want fairies," said Dana.

"I'd want extra icing," said Patty.

Marian leaned in for a closer look. "I like the bride and groom, but I think they should be wearing bathing suits and standing on a desert island."

Julia looked thoughtful. "I like the cake just the way it is. That's the exact cake I want when I get married."

"What about you, Peter?" Adele asked. "What do you think should be on top of the cake?"

"Tail," he replied, predictably. "Tail in a wedding dress."

During Tail's first trip to the new animal hospital on Sixteenth Street, the vet had informed the Burleys that their cat was a girl.

They crossed Sixth Avenue and turned onto Tenth Street, Adele setting a leisurely pace — unlike Abby, Dana couldn't help thinking. Dana's mother always seemed to be in a great big hurry. But Adele wandered along, stopping at shop windows and asking the children about all sorts of things, except school.

"What do you think is the best age to be?" she wanted to know. And later, "If you could invent a new kind of weather, what would it be?"

They found an abandoned hopscotch court on the sidewalk in front of a brownstone, and Adele tossed a pebble and jumped along to the other end, the girls and Peter following, Peter jumping heavily in every square with two feet.

At last they reached the park, sweaty and out of breath.

"This must be the hottest day of the year so far," said Adele.

Julia fanned herself with her hand. "Our teachers opened every window in school."

"And a bee flew in our room and landed on Mrs. Jefferson's head!" exclaimed Patty.

"Look! Ice cream!" shouted Peter.

Sure enough, the Good Humor truck was standing near the entrance to the park.

"Peter can always spot ice cream," said Adele. She began to search through her pocketbook. "Anybody want a Good Humor?"

"Yes!" cried Dana and Julia and Peter and Marian and Patty.

Dana's ice cream began to drip down her fingers the moment she unwrapped her strawberry shortcake bar. She licked it fiercely.

They walked around the park then, all six of them slurping away. They watched two squirrels racing in spirals up a gingko tree. They watched children on the swings and the slides and the monkey bars. They watched old men sitting on benches and reading the newspaper, dogs on leashes, and a mother hovering around her little boy, who was zooming a wooden plane through the air.

"Don't go near the garbage can!" the mother cried. "Don't put your hand in your mouth! Stay away from the litter! You'll catch polio."

Julia looked nervously at her aunt. "You can catch polio from litter? Is it that easy?"

Dana thought of the pictures she'd seen of children

who had contracted polio, crippled children with braces on their legs, and one terrifying photo of a girl exactly her age, who was spending her life inside an iron lung, which now did her breathing for her. She would never get out of the lung, Marian had told her. It would have to breathe for her forever, even when she was an old lady, if she lived that long.

"You're not going to get polio," said Adele. "Don't touch the litter, wash your hands often, and keep them out of your mouth."

Julia looked down at her nearly finished ice-cream cone. "I'm holding the cone in my hand!" she wailed.

"Don't worry so much about everything," said Dana. "We'll wash our hands when we're done."

"But by then it will be too late."

Dana sighed. "Come on. Let's rinse off our hands in the water fountain."

She crossed the park, the others following her, and stood behind three girls waiting in line at a stone water fountain. When it was her turn, she stuck her hands, one at a time, under the stream of water, shook them off, and wiped them on the skirt of her plaid dress. Julia rinsed off her hands, then Patty rinsed hers off, and that was when Dana noticed the mother and the little boy with the airplane again.

The mother was watching them, brow furrowed, lips set in a disapproving line. "That water is for drinking," she said. "You're getting your germs all over the fountain." It was Peter's turn to wash his hands and the woman stared at him for a moment, and then grabbed her son's wrist and pulled him away, looking over her shoulder at Peter and shaking her head.

Dana glanced at her aunt, who took Peter by one wet hand and led him toward the benches at the edge of the park. "Let's sit for a moment," Adele said to the girls. "We'll dry off and cool off, and then you can go play."

Marian and Patty obediently sat squished together on a bench, and Patty withdrew a grimy length of string from the pocket of her skirt. "Let's play cat's cradle," she said, and looped the string around her hands.

"Me first!" cried Marian.

Despite herself, Julia leaned in for a closer look.

Dana turned to Adele. "Did Dad tell you the news?" she asked.

"Your mom said you had news but that you'd probably want to tell me yourself. What is it?"

Dana clasped her hands together. "Dad is starting a new book and it needs illustrations. Guess who's going to draw them."

Adele raised her eyebrows. "You?"

Dana nodded. "I'm going to get paid! I even had to sign a contract. The book is called *Father*, and the cover will say, 'By Zander Burley, with illustrations by Dana Burley.'"

"Honey, that's wonderful!" exclaimed Adele, and she put her arms around Dana. "What kind of illustrations does the book need?"

"I think Dad said they're called spots. Some of them are more like decorations. They're small. I'm going to do them in pen and ink. I'm not used to pen and ink, though, so Mrs. Booth is going to give me private lessons over the summer. But all the art in the book will be mine, with no help from anyone. The book will be a family affair — that's what Dad said. A book called *Father* with illustrations by the author's daughter. Get it?"

"I do. You are an amazing person, Dana."

"Thank you," said Dana, who could feel her cheeks flaming but was pleased nevertheless.

"I swing now?" asked Peter, who had been sitting placidly on the bench next to Adele.

Patty and Marian turned away from the string game. "Please? Can we go play?"

"Sure," Adele replied. "Go ahead."

"Let's play freeze tag," said Julia.

"Oh, look. The swings are free!" cried Patty. "Come on!"

Dana took Peter by the hand and followed Patty and Marian to the swings. She glanced over her shoulder at her sister. "We'll play freeze tag next," she said kindly. "I promise. Come on. Swing with us."

Two regular swings and one baby swing were free, all in a row. Patty and Marian claimed the regular swings, and Dana helped Peter into the baby swing. He was too big for the baby swings now, but he had fallen off the other swings several times, and Abby and Zander had proclaimed that he would have to use the swings with the seat backs and the bars until his balance improved.

Dana slid the bar down the chains until it was just above Peter's lap. "Hold on," she told him. "Hold on tight." When she noticed that Peter's brown oxfords were dragging in the scuffed, dusty earth below the swings, she added, "Pick up your feet."

Peter obliged and Dana began to push him slowly.

"Faster," commanded Peter.

Dana pushed harder. At the edge of her vision she caught sight of the mother and her boy.

"I want to swing," said the boy.

"All the swings are taken," his mother replied. She raised her voice. "Those swings are for little children," she called to

Dana. "Get him out and let him wait his turn for the other swings."

Dana ignored her. She pushed even harder, and Peter began to laugh. "More!" he called.

The woman watched, hands on hips.

Dana had pushed Peter twice more when she realized that he was suddenly very quiet. "Everything all right?" she called to him.

Her brother let out a groan.

"Peter?"

Nothing. And then, as the swing began its arc back toward Dana, Peter groaned again and a long, slobbery trail of vomit whooshed from his mouth as he barfed up his ice cream bar.

"Gross!" shrieked Patty and Marian, and they jumped to the ground, out of barf range.

Dana caught the back of Peter's swing and brought it to a stop.

"Oh no," she said as Peter leaned over the side of the swing and vomited again.

The mother, who had been waiting nearby with her little boy, said, as if finishing a conversation she had begun with Dana, "And that is exactly why children like him should stay at home, where they belong."

Adele was at Peter's side in an instant. She glared at the woman, and Dana could see her mouth working, but then her aunt turned away and helped Peter out of the swing instead. "Come on," she said to the girls. "Time to go."

"Just a minute," said Dana. She walked under the swing set and stopped a few feet from the woman. "My brother couldn't help getting sick. He didn't do anything wrong. He's just a little kid. And I think you are very rude to say something like that in front of him. He can understand what you say, you know. I thought adults weren't supposed to be rude. Especially not to children. My parents taught my sister and brother and me not to be rude. But I guess nobody taught you that."

Dana sensed she might have gone a bit too far (she hoped she wasn't being rude, after all), but she would not apologize for her words. The woman needed to hear them. She waited until the woman had turned away and led her son quietly in the direction of the gate to the park. Then she ran to Adele, who was wiping Peter's face, and she took her brother's hand and held it tightly.

Chapter 6

Dana was awakened from a deep and luxurious sleep by a knock on her door. She groaned, rolled over in bed, and peered at her alarm clock. Six thirty.

"What?" she called. "It's six thirty."

"Time for school!" came Peter's voice.

Dana groaned again. "No. There's no school today, Peter. I told you that last night. Today is Thanksgiving."

"But it's Thursday."

Dana was impressed with her little brother. "How do you know that?" she called, interested in spite of the early hour.

"From my teacher. Can I come in?"

"Sure." Dana sat up, stuffed her pillow behind her, leaned against it, and flicked on her lamp.

The door opened and Peter entered her room. He was dressed in corduroy pants, a white shirt, a yellow sweater, and his brown oxfords, the laces untied. "See? I'm all ready."

"You look very nice, but there's still no school today. Just like on Saturday and Sunday."

"Today is Thursday. *Thursday.* Yesterday at Circle Time my teacher said it was Wednesday. So today is Thursday."

"I know. But remember the paper turkey you made? And the story your teacher told you about the Pilgrims?"

"Yes."

"That's because of Thanksgiving. Which is today. And Thanksgiving is a special holiday."

Peter considered this. "Is tomorrow Friday?"

"Yes, tomorrow is Friday. But there's no school then either. Not until Monday."

"I like school," Peter declared, and left the room.

Peter did indeed like school. He was seven years old now, and enrolled in his first year at Wings Academy, which was a private school for children with mental retardation. Dana's mother had worried that Peter wasn't ready for this big step, but on September 16th, he had walked through the doorway to his classroom for the first time, waved briefly to Abby, taken his teacher's hand, and entered the world of school. He was learning the days of the week, how to count, and the names of colors, and he came home at the end of each day with paintings and large sheets of widely lined paper on which he practiced writing the alphabet with a fat blue pencil.

Peter knocked on Dana's door again and stuck his head back in her room. "It's snowing!" he announced. "Snow is a kind of weather."

Dana peeked outside. It wasn't just snowing. It looked like a blizzard. She could barely see across the street. She threw back her covers and ran barefoot down to the second floor, passed her parents' bedroom, and continued to the first floor and into the living room, where she found her parents side by side, watching the storm.

"How much snow do we have?" asked Dana.

"Too much," said her mother, shaking her head.

"Six inches," said her father.

"That's not so bad." Dana sniffed the air. "You're already cooking," she said to Abby. "I can smell the turkey."

Abby held up crossed fingers. She had been preparing food for days, with help from a part-time cook. The refrigerator was jammed with vegetables and olives and cranberries and mysterious foil-covered dishes. Adele was coming for dinner, and so were ten guests, and the affair was to be very fancy. Dana and Julia had new velvet dresses with lace collars (Dana's dress was black, Julia's was red), and Peter had a new suit.

"I just·hope everyone can make it," said Abby.

"They'll make it," said Zander. "They can always take the subway. There's no blizzard underground."

That may have been true, but by eleven o'clock, the two women hired to help Abby in the kitchen that day were an hour late. Dana's mother began to wring her hands.

"We can help you," said Dana, shutting her sketchbook.

"We'll all pitch in," added Zander. "What do you want us to do?"

The Burleys gathered in the kitchen and Abby assigned them tasks. Ten minutes later Dana and Peter were setting the table in the dining room with silver and fine china, when the doorbell rang and the two women hustled inside, apologies trailing behind them with their snowy footprints.

Dana's mother breathed a sigh of relief.

The guests had been invited for a two o'clock dinner. Adele arrived at one thirty, which Dana took as a good sign, but then an hour passed and the bell didn't ring again.

"Is it very slippery outside?" Abby asked. Dana, Julia, and Peter put their outdoor clothes on over their fancy ones and stepped outside in the fog and snow and wet air. They made their way to the sidewalk and tried sliding on it.

"It's only a little slippery," Dana reported, a few minutes

later, as she and her brother and sister stood dripping slush in the front hall.

"And the snow is stopping," added Julia.

Half an hour passed and the first guests finally arrived, trailing apologies of their own behind them. By three thirty everyone was gathered in the living room with drinks. Dana, Julia, and Peter passed around plates of hors d'oeuvres (which Peter called "orders"), and Dana dutifully curtsied each time anyone said "thank you" to her. The guests (not counting Adele) were five women and five men, and three of the men and one of the women were famous writers of books for grown-ups. Dana wished her father knew Eleanor Estes or Dr. Seuss, who wrote books for children, but he did not. Still, she felt pleased, as she always did, to chat with people who had written novels that she saw stacked in the windows of bookstores. And her cheeks flamed with pride when Ben Thomas, who wrote great fat books about scandalous families, said to her, "I hear you're going to illustrate your father's next book. Would you share some of your work with us?"

Dana was on the way to her bedroom to retrieve the box containing her drawings when she heard a shriek from below. She turned and ran back downstairs to find half the guests hurrying into the kitchen.

"What happened?" she asked Julia.

"I don't know. Something in the kitchen."

This was when Dana saw a plume of smoke puffing out of the kitchen door and winding through the dining room. "The turkey's on fire!" she heard Ben Thomas exclaim.

Dana felt her heart begin to pound, even though she realized that several of the guests were laughing. She stood on tiptoe to peer through the small crowd of people at the kitchen door and saw the flaming turkey sitting in a basting pan on the table. One of the women who was helping Abby was fanning the turkey with a dish towel, and the other was trying to douse it with a teacup full of water.

"Stand back!" ordered Dana's father, just as if he were a character in one of his own books. He grabbed a fire extinguisher from the cupboard and aimed it at the turkey.

"No!" cried Dana's mother.

She was too late.

With a whoosh of white foam, the flames disappeared.

"It's out," said Ben, looking at the dripping, ruined mess in the pan.

"Zander!" Dana's mother exclaimed. "What —" Her voice was drowned out by more laughter. "I really don't see what's so funny," she said.

"Come on. It is a *little* funny," said Zander.

Dana looked from her mother to her father. "But what are we going to eat? We have to have turkey on Thanksgiving."

Her father smiled. "Not this Thanksgiving."

Dana felt a hand on her shoulder and turned around. Adele drew her away from the crowd at the doorway. "It's okay, honey. There's plenty of other food. And the guests have a sense of humor about what happened."

"But Mom is upset, and I just know she and Dad are going to have a fight —"

"Dana?"

Dana turned to see Peter standing at the foot of the staircase, tears running down his cheeks. She rushed to her brother and put her arms around him. "It's okay," she said. "The fire is out."

"Fire?" Peter frowned. Then he said, "I can't find Tail."

"What do you mean? When was the last time you saw her?"

"I don't know. But I can't find her now. I looked and looked."

"Did you look under your bed?"

"Yes."

"In Julia's closet?"

"Yes."

"Did you look on the chair in your dad's study?" asked Adele.

Peter sniffled. "Yes."

"We'd better have a search, then," said Julia, who had left the group of people exclaiming over the turkey. "Maybe all the excitement scared Tail."

"Everyone choose a floor and search carefully," said Adele.

Fifteen minutes later, when they met up on the first floor, there was still no sign of Tail, and Peter was crying noisily. "She's gone!" he wailed.

"I'm sure she isn't actually gone," said Dana's mother reasonably. "Nobody would have let her out of the house. She has to be here somewhere. Let's look again."

"But we looked *every*where," sobbed Peter.

"No, we didn't," said Dana, brightening. "I know one place we didn't search. The kitchen."

Peter made a beeline for the kitchen, with Dana, Julia, Adele, Abby, and Zander at his heels. From the living room came the clinking of glasses and more loud laughter, so Dana knew the guests were entertaining themselves. The Burleys and Adele peered under chairs and into improbable places, such as the tiny space behind the refrigerator, but there was still no sign of Tail.

At last Peter opened a cupboard. Dana was about to say, "Peter, how could Tail have gotten into a closed cupboard?"

when her brother exclaimed, "Oh! Oh, here she is! But there's . . . Uh-oh. Come here."

"What's wrong?" asked Zander.

Everyone crowded around the cupboard. There, nestled on a pile of dish towels, were Tail and four tiny, damp kittens.

"Kittens?" said Abby. "Now, how did she . . . I mean, when —"

"She *has* been looking kind of fat," said Julia.

"I know, but I just thought we were feeding her too much."

"What do we do now?" asked Dana.

"Let's find a basket," her father replied.

Tail was remarkably calm about being moved from her hidden bed to a basket in Peter's room. Dana's parents and Adele returned to the guests, but Dana, Julia, and Peter remained crowded around the basket until finally they were called downstairs to a Thanksgiving dinner, which consisted of vegetables and bologna with all the trimmings.

"I don't even mind about the turkey now," Dana told Adele. "Not since we found the kittens."

"And I thought the snow was going to be our biggest problem today," said Abby.

"The kittens aren't a problem," Julia replied.

"You know what I mean. This isn't quite the Thanksgiving we had planned." Abby looked around at the guests. "I remember another Thanksgiving that didn't go as planned," she went on. "I was eight years old."

Dana turned to her aunt. "Were you born yet?" she asked.

"Nope. Not for another five years or so."

"What happened, Mommy?" Julia wanted to know.

"Snow again," Abby replied. "There was a blizzard and the power went out and the phones, too. We lived in a very rural area, so our guests — they were our cousins — weren't able to travel to our house. We had to eat all that food by ourselves."

"That was in the olden days, right, Mom?" asked Dana.

"It did seem like the olden days. We had kerosene lamps and a potato bin and an icebox that kept food cold with blocks of ice."

"Your mother is actually four hundred years old," said Zander, and everyone laughed.

Dana cut up a slice of bologna. She thought about the turkey fire and about Tail and her kittens, and she decided that when she was grown up, she would tell her children about this Thanksgiving Day, and about the story her own mother had told of another Thanksgiving, which was so long ago, it might have taken place in a different world.

Chapter 7

Friday, February 14th, 1958

Dana stood before her closet and surveyed the clothes hanging in it. She pulled out a red jumper and a white blouse and considered them. She hung them up again. She pulled out a red-and-pink-striped dress and considered it. She hung it up again. Why, she thought, hadn't she chosen her outfit the night before? Today was Valentine's Day and there would be a party at school. She wanted to look perfect for it.

"Dana?" She heard her sister's voice from the hallway. "What are you wearing today?"

"I don't know yet."

"Could we maybe be samesies?"

Dana sighed. "What do you want to wear?"

"The red dresses that Mommy bought us at Best's."

Dana let out a sigh of relief. "I got ink on mine," she reported truthfully. "I'll have to wear something else."

Dana pulled out the jumper and blouse again and put them on in a hurry. She didn't want to be late for school on

Valentine's Day. This was one of her favorite days of the year. She and Julia had spent every evening that week making Valentines for their classmates. And in school the day before, their teacher had allowed them to close their arithmetic books half an hour early in order to make heart-shaped pouches to hang on their desks. Into these pouches would be delivered their Valentine cards, and during the party, the twins would open the cards and read them while they ate cupcakes and tried not to look at Abby, who was one of the room mothers that year.

"Girls!" Dana could hear her father call from downstairs. "Peter! Come on. You don't want to be late."

Dana flew down the stairs behind Julia, Peter stumping down behind them more deliberately. They found that their father had strung red streamers above the kitchen table and that a box of conversation hearts had been placed on each of their chairs.

Dana opened her box instantly and shook a candy onto the palm of her hand. The pink letters on the yellow heart spelled *HUG ME*.

"Be mine," said Julia.

Peter withdrew a heart from his box. "F-I-R-S-T," he read slowly, "K-I-S-S." He frowned. "What does that make?"

"It spells *first kiss*," said Dana.

Peter clapped his hand over his mouth. "Eww!" He pretended to faint on the floor.

Dana and Julia ran into school that day, each carrying a bag containing the Valentines they'd made. They hung their coats in a hurry and then walked around their classroom, going from desk to desk and dropping their cards into the pouches. Each time Dana passed her own pouch, she checked it to see how fat it was getting. Her fingers itched to take the envelopes out and count them, but she knew she was supposed to wait for the party.

"Isn't this the longest day in the world?" Patty said to her at recess that afternoon, and Dana groaned in agreement.

But the wait was almost over. The moment the bell rang, they ran back to their classroom and the party began. Dana and Julia's mother, Marian's mother, and Daniel Wright's mother were standing woodenly at the back of the room, presiding over the cupcakes and punch. Abby waved just once to the twins, so that was all right. Dana breathed a sigh of relief as she slid into her seat.

"Class," said Mrs. Sullivan, their teacher, when the room was quiet, "you may open your Valentines."

In a flash the pouches were emptied and Dana began to tear open her stack of envelopes. She was reading a card from Marian that showed a kitten wearing a pair of rain boots above the words, *Bet your boots, I'm the one for you,* when her mother placed a pink-frosted cupcake on her desk. A moment later Daniel's mother handed her a cup of red punch.

This is perfect, thought Dana. *Absolutely perfect.* She sipped her punch and licked frosting from the cupcake and opened another Valentine.

The perfect day continued at home that afternoon. February 14th was not only Valentine's Day, but Adele's birthday. Their aunt had been given the afternoon off from the costume shop, and she arrived at Dana's shortly after the twins and Peter returned from school.

"Happy birthday!" cried all five Burleys when Adele entered the town house.

Peter tugged on her sleeve and asked solemnly, "How old are you?"

"Peter! It isn't polite to ask a grown-up how old she is," said Julia.

Adele waved her hand. "Oh, I don't care. I'm twenty-three, Peter."

Peter pretended to faint again. Then he lay on the couch in the living room where he was soon joined by Tail and Tail's one remaining kitten. The other three kittens had recently been given away — one to Marian's family, one to Ben Thomas, and the third to a neighbor down the street. Peter had cried as each one left and begged to keep the fourth. Dana's parents had finally relented, which was how Squeaky had joined the family.

Dana and Julia each took one of Adele's hands and led her into the living room. They sat her in an armchair and said, "Wait right here." When they returned, they were carrying a bag of gifts, and Adele spent the next half hour opening them while various Burleys exclaimed, "I made that!" or "You wouldn't believe how long I had to look to find just the right one."

Adele left shortly before five o'clock to spend the evening with friends. Dana's mother surveyed the mess of wrapping paper on the floor. "Let's clean this up," she said, "and then it's time to get ready for Mrs. Burger."

"Mrs. Burger?" said Dana. She had forgotten that she and Julia and Peter were to have a babysitter that night.

"Really? Mrs. Burger?" cried Julia.

The twins loved Mrs. Burger because she was teaching them to play poker. Peter loved her because she read Uncle Wiggily stories to him and kept Life Savers in her pockets.

"Yes," said their mother. "She'll be here at six. Your dad and I are going to Ben's party tonight."

"A fancy party?" asked Dana with interest. "A publishing party?"

Her mother nodded. "At the Waldorf. Ben's new book has just come out. It's a big deal."

"Are you going to wear a gown?" Julia wanted to know.

"Well, not a gown. But my new dress. The green one."

"With the sparkles?" said Dana. "Ooh, glamorous!"

"Mommy?" said Peter, who was still lying on the couch. "I don't feel good."

Abby was at Peter's side in an instant. "You don't?" She put her hand on his forehead. "Oh dear. I think you have a fever."

"My froat hurts."

"Let me take a look." Dana's mother hurried out of the living room and returned with a flashlight and a thermometer. She peered into Peter's throat. "It does look red," she said. "Let's see what your temperature is." She stuck the thermometer under Peter's tongue and checked her watch. Three minutes later she removed the thermometer. "A hundred and one," she said, and clucked her tongue. "I wonder what's brewing. Zander!" she called. "Come here for a sec. Peter's sick. I won't be able to go tonight."

Dana's father appeared in the doorway, looking worried. "What's the matter, buddy?"

"My froat hurts."

"His temperature is a hundred and one," Abby added.

Zander frowned. "That isn't so bad," he said. "Mrs. Burger can handle this."

Abby shook her head. "No. I don't want to leave him."

"But, honey, tonight is important. Ben is one of my best friends. We can't back out of this now."

"You don't have to back out. Go without me. Just let me call Mrs. Burger so I can catch her before she leaves her apartment."

"Honey —" said Zander. But Abby was already dialing the phone. Dana's father put his hand on Peter's shoulder. "I'm sorry you don't feel well."

"Me, too," said Peter.

Suddenly Zander smiled. "Hey," he said to Dana and Julia. "How would you two like to be my dates tonight?"

"Really?" cried Dana. "You mean we get to go to the fancy party? Oh yes!"

"But," said Julia, "Mrs. Burger was going to play poker with us."

"But she isn't coming now," said Dana.

"I know, but . . . I kind of wanted to watch *Leave It to Beaver* tonight. I looked it up in the *TV Guide*. It's a new one. Something about the Beaver and a bank account."

Dana gaped at her sister. "You mean you'd rather stay home and watch *Leave It to Beaver* than go to a party at the Waldorf Astoria Hotel?"

Julia shrugged. "Is it okay if I don't go?" she asked her father.

"I guess so."

"I can't believe you're going to miss this!" exclaimed Dana. "You'd get to dress up and stay out late."

"You go," said Julia.

Zander turned to Dana. "Okay, pumpkin. You'll be my date. Hurry and get ready."

Dana flew upstairs to her room. Even though it was Valentine's Day, she chose her black velvet Thanksgiving dress, the one with the lace collar. It was the fanciest dress she owned. She pulled on a pair of white tights, brushed her hair fifty times, swept it back from her face, and tied it with a black ribbon. Then she clattered downstairs in her patent leather Mary Janes and ran to her father, who was wearing his very best suit.

"Ready!" she announced.

Dana felt like a princess later that evening when she entered the ballroom at the Waldorf Astoria, her arm linked through her father's. Several people turned to smile at them, and

Dana smiled back serenely, the way she felt an actual princess might smile. When they approached Ben Thomas, who was talking with a group of important-looking men, he clapped Zander on the back and then said, "Dana, what a pleasant surprise! Look, everyone. Zander's date tonight is his daughter. This is Dana Burley, and she's illustrating her father's latest book. When does it come out, Zander? In June?"

A waiter approached them, carrying a tray full of crystal glasses. He handed one to Zander. "Champagne, sir," he said. He turned to Dana. "And you, madam? May I bring you a Shirley Temple?"

"Oh yes. Please."

The waiter returned with Dana's Shirley Temple — ginger ale and sweet-tasting grenadine with many ice cubes, three cherries, and a red plastic swizzle stick. Dana sipped it daintily.

All evening she walked around the ballroom with her father, saying hello to his friends, answering questions about *Father*, sipping her cocktail, and sampling hors d'oeuvres proffered to her on silver trays. Zander looped Dana's arm through his as if she truly were his date. He pointed out famous guests and whispered stories about them that made Dana giggle. Important publishing people approached them and clapped Zander on the shoulder, and Zander clapped them back. His words grew a little loud, because the waiters, who were always circulating the room in their tuxes ("penguin suits," Zander called them), kept offering him full glasses of champagne or asking if he wanted a cocktail — and Zander kept saying yes.

"Daddy?" Dana said. She was about to add, "Are you sure you should have another drink?" because she wasn't at all certain that she could hail a cab by herself, which was what she felt she might have to do if her father's voice grew wobbly and his legs got rubbery.

But just as the words were about to leave her mouth, Zander set down his glass and left it on a table. Dana heaved an inward sigh of relief. Arm in arm, she and her father continued their tour of the room.

The first time Dana looked at the clock on the wall, it read eleven thirty, which was the latest she had ever stayed up on a night that wasn't New Year's Eve. By the time she and Zander drew up in front of their town house, Dana nodding on her father's shoulder, it was after midnight.

"Bedtime for you," said Zander, helping her out of the cab.

Dana fell into bed five minutes later, certain that she was a character in a fairy tale.

Chapter 8

Winter was over. The days had grown warm and sticky again, and New York City panted in the heavy air and unrelenting sunshine.

"I'm glad school's out," said Julia. She and Dana and Peter were sprawled on the steps to their town house, fanning themselves with red-tasseled, flowered fans that they had bought at Hop Kee's on an excursion to Chinatown. "It's too hot for school."

"School's out! School's out! Teacher wore her bloomers out!" sang Peter. He had successfully completed his first year at Wings Academy, and could now write his name and count to sixteen, and had also made up a poem, which went: *Tail is nice. She likes mice. Tail is fine. She is mine.* Peter could cut with scissors and make his own lunch and tie his laces, and he had a friend, Sal, who was in his class at Wings and lived just two streets away.

"Are you glad school is over?" Julia asked Peter.

Peter looked thoughtful. "No," he said finally. "I just sang the song because it's funny. I like school. Next year we go on a field trip."

"Where?" Dana wanted to know.

Peter shrugged. "We get to ride on a bus."

Julia withdrew a hankie from the pocket of her dress and wiped her forehead. "How hot do you think it is? A hundred?"

"Probably," said Dana.

"Maybe Mommy would let us play in the yard with the hose."

"Nope. Too late. It's almost time to get ready."

"Get ready for what?" asked Peter.

"For the big party tonight."

"Another party? Is Mrs. Burger coming?"

Dana laughed. "There *have* been a lot of parties lately. But, no, Mrs. Burger isn't coming this time."

"Why not?"

"Because we're *all* going to the party."

"All of us? Really?"

Dana nodded. "It's at the Plaza Hotel. It's the party for Dad's new book, the one I illustrated. I mean, the one I drew the pictures for. The book is all finished, and Dad and I are going to sign copies for the guests." Dana glanced at her sister, who had moved four steps down and had begun a solitary game of jacks. "You get to wear your suit, Peter. It's going to be really fun."

He jumped to his feet and began flapping his hands. "My suit! And a tie? And my new shoes?"

Peter loved nothing better than dressing up.

"Yes. All those things. Come on. We'd better go inside. Mom wants us to get ready."

Julia groaned. "Now? But we don't have to leave for two hours."

"She wants us to take baths."

Another groan from Julia.

"Don't you want to go?" Dana asked her, although she knew the answer, and tried to put herself in Julia's position. If she were the one who had to go to a party where her twin sister was going to be the center of attention, she would probably feel jealous, too. Which was why she refrained from adding, "Is *Leave It to Beaver* on tonight?" and instead said, "I know it's going to be a long evening, but it should be fun. Dad said famous people will be there."

"You mean besides you?" muttered Julia.

Dana stood up and took Peter's hand. "I'll help you run the bath," she told him.

This time when Dana's father said, "Our chariot awaits," he didn't mean a taxi. He opened the door to the town house and ushered the very dressed-up Burleys down the steps to a waiting limousine.

"Ooh!" said Peter softly. "This is very fancy. Very, very fancy. Now be careful, everybody. And be polite. Remember your manners. Hey!" He stood back from the car and began to count. "One, two, three doors on this side. Three doors! This is the biggest car in the world."

The limo driver was standing woodenly by the car, white-gloved hands at his sides. He opened the doors for Dana and her family. Dana found a seat inside, once again feeling like a princess. She glanced at Julia, saw that her sister was grinning, and switched places so that she could sit next to her. "Pretend we're princesses," she said, and Julia's smile widened.

"We're on our way to the ball," her twin replied.

"Wait until we get to the Plaza. Then we'll really feel like princesses."

"I wish I had a crown," said Peter.

As the car slithered through the busy streets of Manhattan, Dana and Julia and Peter waved out the windows to people on the sidewalks. Abby and Zander sat at the back of the car, holding hands and smiling. When the car drew up in front of the grand Plaza Hotel, Julia said, "Here's our castle."

Peter replied, "Really? This is a castle?"

"No, just pretend," Dana told him. "But it does look like a castle."

The Burleys climbed out of the limo and Dana tipped her head back to look up, up, up at the twenty-story chateau, with its angled green roof, flags flapping in the breeze. Then Zander took Abby by the elbow and the Burleys walked up the wide steps to a uniformed doorman, who ushered them inside.

"Oh," said Dana, under her breath, as she gazed at the chandeliers and rich carpets and marble floors.

"It *is* a castle," said Peter. "It really is."

Zander led the Burleys into the Grand Ballroom, where Dana stood for a few moments in her white lace dress, then turned in a circle, surveying the guests and the tuxedoed waiters and the silver trays of food until she began to feel dizzy.

"Ah! Zander! The man of the hour!" Dana heard someone proclaim. "And there's the lovely and talented Dana."

"Saul," said Dana's father, a smile spreading across his face. "This is my daughter Julia and my son, Peter. You already know Abby and Dana. This is Saul Marks, my editor."

Peter stuck out his hand and Saul shook it.

"What's an editor?" asked Peter.

"Now, that is a very good question. An editor," Saul began to explain, but he was interrupted by a waiter who approached the Burleys and then stood stock-still, hands behind his back. Zander turned and the waiter said, "Excuse me, but I wanted to know if I could get you anything to drink." He bowed to Dana and Julia. "We have Shirley Temples, if you're interested. And for you, sir," he said to Peter, "a Roy Rogers."

"Oh yes!" cried Dana. "Julia, you have to have a Shirley Temple! It's just like a real cocktail, with cherries and ice cubes and everything. But what's a Roy Rogers?" she asked the waiter.

"It's cola with syrup and cherries. Very tasty."

"Do you want one, Peter?" asked Dana.

"Yes!" exclaimed Peter, who had forgotten about his question for Saul.

The waiter hurried away.

"Dad? Can we walk around by ourselves?" asked Dana. "Julia and I will watch Peter."

"Sure, sure," replied Zander, reaching for the adult cocktail the waiter handed him, and ignoring Abby's warning look.

The last thing Dana heard her mother say as she hurried off with her brother and sister was "Don't overdo it tonight, Zander."

"Look!" cried Julia a few moments later, Shirley Temple in hand. "That lady in the gold dress. She's famous. Isn't she? I think I saw her on television."

"Oh, and there's Eva Montague," said Dana. "She's somebody. Wow, this is amazing."

"What's that?" asked Peter, pointing across the room to a long table with a pyramid of books stacked on one end.

"I guess that's where Dad and I are going to have our signing. Those are copies of *Father*."

Julia said flatly, "Let's go get something to eat," and she turned away.

"Dana! Come have your picture taken with us." Dana felt a hand at her elbow, and she looked up into Saul's lined face.

"Sure," she said. "Julia. Peter. Come here."

"No, no," said Saul. "We want a photo of the author, the editor, and the illustrator."

"But —" said Dana.

"There'll be time for family photos later."

Dana watched Julia drift off in the direction of their mother, Peter holding on to the sash of her dress, his Roy Rogers sloshing over the side of the glass.

The evening swirled by. Dana found her brother and sister again and they decided to sample every single thing that went by on a tray.

"Ew!" cried Julia as she sampled a chunk of pickled watermelon, but then she reached for another.

"Hmm," said Peter, swallowing a cracker piled with what looked like bright orange pearls.

"More caviar?" the waiter asked him.

"No, thank you," said Peter politely. "Dana, do you have a napkin?"

Dana was looking for the waiter whose tray was laden with the teensy cakes he had said were called petit fours, when her father made his way to her through the crowd. "It's time, pumpkin," he said. "Ready?"

"I guess so. I'm nervous."

"Don't be. All you have to do is sign your name. And smile a lot."

Dana, Julia, and Peter followed their father to the table with the pyramid of books.

"Ah! There they are," said Saul, who was standing behind the table. "Zander, you sit there, and, Dana, you sit next to him. Each of the guests will be given a copy of the book. They'll wait on line for their turn to meet you and to have the book signed. And that's it. We should be done in about two hours."

"Two *hours*?" exclaimed Dana. She looked at the line that was starting to form and at the huge crowd of people still laughing and talking and eating. "Okay," she said. "We'd better get started."

The very first person in line — an unsmiling woman who, to Dana's fascination, was wearing a silver tiara in her piled-up blond hair — handed her copy of *Father* to Zander and said, "I hope this is as good as the rest of your books."

Zander cleared his throat. "Well, I hope so, too." He passed the book to Dana. "This is my daughter Dana, the illustrator."

Dana carefully printed her name under Zander's signature and handed the book back to the woman. She glanced helplessly at her father. "Um, I hope you enjoy it," she said, and the woman's face softened.

"I'm sure I will," she said. "Thank you."

Dana signed her name so often that night that her wrist began to ache. But each time she handed a book back to a pair of outstretched hands, she said, "Thank you for coming," or "I hope you enjoy it," or "It was nice to meet you," and she remembered to smile.

Saul disappeared at some point, then returned with two glasses of water, which he placed on the table between Dana and her father. Dana didn't have time to reach for hers. She continued signing and smiling and saying thank you, and when, eventually, she leaned over to peer at her father's wristwatch, she was amazed to see that it was almost midnight.

"Dad!" she cried. "Look how late it is."

She glanced around the ballroom and saw that most of the guests were leaving. In a chair against the wall not far away sat Dana's mother, Peter dozing in her lap. Julia was in a chair next to them, sound asleep, head tipped back against the wall, her hair ribbon dangling down the side of her face.

"I think we're about done here," Saul said at last.

Dana barely remembered leaving the Grand Ballroom and climbing inside another waiting limousine. She fell asleep as soon as she had settled into her seat and didn't wake up until she heard her father thanking the driver and urging his tired family onto the sidewalk. Abby carried Peter inside and laid him on his bed, still in his suit.

Dana and Julia stumbled to their rooms. Dana had just closed her door when she heard Julia call from the hallway, "You're going to be famous someday."

Dana opened her door. "What?"

"You're going to be famous. I can already tell. Or else you're going to do something great. But not me. I guess I don't mind, though. I don't think I want to be famous. That's just one of the ways we're different."

"Remember, it's okay to be different. We don't always have to be samesies."

"I know." Julia stooped to pick up Squeaky. She held him to her cheek. "I know."

"Like Mom and Adele," said Dana. "They're not twins, but they're sisters, and look how different they are. They're still really, really close, though. You know what? Tomorrow we should go roller-skating in the park. Just us, okay? It'll be fun."

The look that Julia flashed was so grateful that Dana fell asleep that night feeling guilty, and dreamed of running down a long, dark city street, escaping from a girl who looked exactly like her.

Chapter 9

Sunday, January 11th, 1959

"Why can't I go with you?" Peter wanted to know. He was standing in the front hall at the bottom of the stairs, arms crossed, lower lip trembling.

"I told you, lovey," said Dana's mother. "It's going to be a very late night."

"But Julia and Dana are going."

Abby sighed. "Do you really want to go to a dinner party at Saul's house on Staten Island? That's all we're doing. We aren't going to the Plaza or to Rumpelmayer's."

Dana sat on the bottom step and pulled her brother into her lap. "It's another party for Dad's book. I'm only going because I drew the pictures. And Julia's going because Saul thought that if he invited me, then he had to invite my twin. But I'd rather stay here with you and Mrs. Burger and play card games."

Peter's lip stopped trembling. "Maybe Mrs. Burger will have Bazooka Bubble Gum this time."

"She did the last week," said Dana.

"I better go find my cards," Peter said, and began climbing the stairs, one slow step up at a time, right foot first, the left catching up, the way he had climbed them since he was three years old and had first learned.

When the Burleys were ready to leave, Zander leaned over to Peter, who was seated on the living room sofa with Mrs. Burger, and kissed the top of his head. "Have fun, pardner," he said, since Peter was wearing his holster and cowboy boots and fringed vest. "I love you."

"I love you, too," said Peter. Then he turned to Mrs. Burger. "Go fish."

The party at Saul's house was exciting at first. *Father* had become a best seller overnight and everyone wanted to meet Zander Burley, who was now more famous than ever. Dana and Julia walked among the guests, drinking Shirley Temples, sampling hors d'oeuvres, and answering questions about what it felt like to be a twin and what it felt like to have a famous father. Sometimes a guest would tell Dana she was very talented and ask if she wanted to be an artist when she grew up, and Dana would nod her head seriously.

Dana's father had three cocktails before dinner began, and another one with dinner, followed by several glasses of wine.

"Slow down," Dana heard Abby whisper harshly to him as dessert was being served.

Zander smiled at her in an unfocused way, picked up his spoon, breathed heavily on it, and stuck it on his nose, where, miraculously, it remained even after he had taken his hand away. "Magic!" he proclaimed.

Dana's mother looked away in disgust.

The guests began to leave just after midnight. Dana had almost fallen asleep at the table and had only been startled back into wakefulness when Julia elbowed her in the ribs.

"People are staring at you," Julia had hissed.

"No, they're not. They're staring at Dad."

Dana made a dash for her coat the moment she heard her mother say, "Saul, thank you so much. This has been lovely. We hate to leave, but we'd better catch the ferry. We told the sitter we'd be back by one."

The wind that night was fierce. It whipped Dana's hair into her face as she and her sister and parents arrived at the St. George terminal. "Brrr," she said aloud, stuffing her hands in her pockets.

"Thank goodness," murmured Abby as they boarded the ferry a few minutes later. She put her hand to her mouth, and Dana thought she looked pale.

Zander stepped onto the deck, chose a spot, and stood by the rail, weaving from side to side. Dana realized that his unsteadiness had little to do with the motion of the boat. "Dad?" she said.

"Shalom!" Zander cried gaily.

Dana, one eye on Abby, who was arm in arm with Julia, took her father by the elbow and urged him forward. "Let's go inside."

Zander didn't seem to hear her. "Look what a beeyutiful night it is," he said, positioning himself stubbornly at the rail again.

The wind was now churning Dana's hair like an egg beater and clouds were scudding across the moon. Dana didn't think the night was beautiful at all.

The ferry left the terminal and pulled into Upper New York Bay. It had traveled for less than five minutes when Abby said, "Excuse me, I don't feel very well," and began to make her way to the ladies' room.

"I'll go with you," said Julia. She frowned at her father and added, "You stay here with Daddy, Dana."

"Mom?" Dana called.

"I'll be all right," said Abby.

Dana's father crossed his arms and rested them on the rail as if he had come across an old friend at a restaurant and were leaning in for a chat. He turned his eyes upward to the moon, which was now completely obscured by clouds, and began to sing, "Shine on, shine on, harvest moon, up in the sky!"

"Dad, shh!"

"Something . . . something . . . since June or — Hey! My hat!"

Dana saw the wind lift her father's hat from his head and send it sailing — very, very slowly, it seemed — out over the bay. When her father lurched forward to grab for the hat, this seemed to happen slowly, too. And when he climbed up on the railing, that happened even more slowly, which was why Dana thought she could catch her father before he fell into the churning, frigid water. She thrust her hand out and clutched at the back of his coat, but found that her hand was empty.

Her father had disappeared.

"Dad!" Dana screamed. "Dad!" She turned around. Not many people were riding the ferry at this hour, and most of the passengers were inside, escaping the wind and cold. "Help!" she shouted. "Help me! Mom! Julia!"

*　*　*

Later, Dana could not recall a single detail of the search for her father, even though she was there for the desperate beginning of it. Abby made certain that the twins were hustled off the ferry in Manhattan and, as quickly as possible, delivered into the arms of a stunned Adele, who had taken a taxi she could barely afford to the terminal. Adele hurried the girls into the taxi and jumped in after them. As they pulled away, Dana turned to look out the back window and saw her mother speaking with a policeman. In the distance she could hear rescue boats grinding their way across the bay.

"Mommy was barfing and barfing in the bathroom," Julia whispered to Dana.

Dana stared at her. "Dad is *gone*," she said. "Don't you understand that?"

The taxi wound through the quiet streets of lower Manhattan. Dana, sitting between Julia and Adele, stared out the window. Adele reached for her hand and Dana snatched it away. Then she felt small and mean, and offered her hand back to her aunt and took Julia's hand as well.

When the cab drew up in front of their house, Dana saw Mrs. Burger framed in the lighted doorway, waiting. She ushered everyone inside. Adele opened her purse. "I don't think I have quite enough —" she started to say.

Mrs. Burger waved her hand away. "Put that back. I don't want it. And I'm staying tonight. What do you want me to do?"

Adele took off her coat and sank onto the couch in the living room. "Well, let me think. I suppose I should call Rose —" She broke off and glanced at the twins. "Could you put the girls to bed, please, Letti?" she asked.

In the midst of Dana's panicked thoughts, she found herself thinking, *Mrs. Burger's first name is Letti.*

"I don't want to go to bed," said Julia.

Mrs. Burger didn't seem to hear her. She stood wordlessly at the bottom of the stairs and waited until the twins began to climb them. Dana felt a weariness overtake her and suddenly thought her legs might not have the strength to carry her to her room, but before she knew it, she was in her nightgown and under the covers, and Mrs. Burger was tucking her in. She looked intently at Dana. "Is there anything you want to ask me?"

"Did Peter win at go fish?"

Mrs. Burger's kind eyes filled with tears. "Yes."

"Okay. Good night."

Despite her weariness, Dana lay awake for a long time that night, straining to hear sounds from below — the ring of the phone, her aunt's voice — but heard only the creaks and groans of the old house, and once, the roar of a motorcycle. She awoke late the next morning, pale January sunshine seeping around the edges of her curtains, when Julia knocked on her door and leaned inside. "Mommy's waiting for you to get up so we can have a family meeting."

"Why?"

"You know why. Come downstairs."

Dana took her time. She didn't want to see anybody's swollen eyes or listen to her mother try to explain to Peter where his father was.

"Dana!" Julia shouted.

"*Okay.* I'm *coming.*"

At the bottom of the stairs Dana bumped into Mrs. Burger, who hugged her and then disappeared into the kitchen. Dana crept into the living room, where her mother, Adele, Julia, and Peter were sitting silently. Peter was wearing his holster again, fingering the silver gun it held, and Dana could see him mouthing, "Stick 'em up," as he looked longingly at it. She squished onto the couch so that she could sit as close to Peter as possible.

For a moment, no one said a word. Then Dana's mother drew in her breath. Her eyes were as swollen as Dana had feared they would be, and Dana looked away from them.

"Peter," Abby began, "there was an accident last night."

"Yeah," said Peter. Then, "An accident?"

"And Daddy is gone."

"Where?"

"I mean, he isn't coming back."

"Why?"

Julia began to tremble. Dana could actually feel her twin's body shuddering.

"Are we sure?" Julia whispered.

Abby nodded. "They found his body."

"Did he drown?" said Julia in another whisper.

"Of course he drowned!" exclaimed Dana. "He fell in the water."

From across the room, Adele said, "Dana, why don't you come here and sit with me?" and Dana crawled gratefully into her aunt's lap.

"Peter, do you understand what's happened?" asked Abby.

Peter nodded. "Daddy fell," he said cheerfully.

"I couldn't catch him," said Dana in a small voice.

Abby swiveled her head around. "Oh no!" she exclaimed. "Oh, Dana, it wasn't your fault. You couldn't have done anything."

Dana looked stonily at her mother. "Maybe *you* could have."

"What?"

"Maybe you could have caught him. You're a grown-up."

"But I . . ."

"I know, I know. You were sick."

Dana heaved herself out of Adele's lap and started for the stairs. Her mother was such a . . . what was the word that had been on her fifth-grade vocabulary list the week before? *Hypocrite?* Her mother was such a hypocrite. All evening she had hounded Dana's father about his drinking, but *she* was the one who had wound up sick in the restroom on the ferry. If *she* hadn't had too much to drink, then *she* would have been at Zander's side when his hat had blown off, and *she* would have caught him or caught the hat, and this day wouldn't be spreading out before Dana like a slow scream.

Dana retreated to her room. She lay across her unmade bed, slipped off her shoes, and hurled them, one at a time, at the door.

Her world had cracked open. The center of her family was gone.

Dana didn't know how she was supposed to proceed with her life.

Chapter 10

Tuesday, August 4th, 1959

"Girls? It's time."

Dana heard her mother's voice and then a knock on her door, followed by a knock on Julia's door.

"Girls?" Abby called again.

"Okay," mumbled Dana. She squinted at her alarm clock. Six fifteen. Then she sat up in a hurry. "Mom?" She flew out of bed and pulled her door open. She found her mother standing by Peter's bed, one hand cradling her huge belly. "Is it really time?" asked Dana, heart pounding. "The baby is coming?"

Dana's mother tried to smile at her, but grimaced instead. She stood very still and drew in a deep breath. Then she let it out slowly. "Yes. The baby is coming. I already called Adele and Mrs. Burger. They'll be here as soon as they can."

"But what should I do?" cried Dana. "Aren't you supposed to lie down or something? Let *me* get Peter up." She looked at her brother, who was lying on his back, one arm flung over the edge of the bed. He was snoring lightly. "Actually, let's just let him sleep. We don't need to wake him."

"He'll want to say good-bye to me," said Abby in a small voice.

This was true. In the months since Zander had died, Peter had begun insisting on knowing where Dana and Julia and their mother were at all times. No one could leave the house without first seeking out Peter and announcing, "I'm just running to the market. I'll be back in half an hour." Or "I'm going over to Marian's house, Peter." The problem was that sometimes Peter forgot what he'd been told, and then tears and accusations were sure to follow. More than once, Dana had entered her house to be greeted by a furious Peter shouting, "Where were you? You didn't tell me you were leaving!"

Dana sighed. "He'll just forget if you say good-bye to him now. He's so sleepy. Don't worry. I'll talk to him when he wakes up."

She closed the door to her brother's room, and she and her mother made their way downstairs.

"Do you have your suitcase?" asked Dana.

Her mother pointed to the front door, where a small brown suitcase (which had been packed for two weeks) was waiting.

"How long have you been up?"

"A few hours. The pains started around midnight."

Dana nodded and looked away. "Do you want anything to eat?" she asked at last.

"No. Thanks. Wait with me, though, will you?"

Dana and her mother sat silently on the living room couch in the early morning light, Dana facing the street so that she could watch for Adele and Mrs. Burger. She was surprised that Julia hadn't come downstairs yet, but her sister's behavior had been unpredictable ever since Abby had tearfully told her and Dana and Peter about their tight finances, and about all the changes that lay ahead for the Burleys.

When five minutes had passed and no one had arrived, Dana turned from the window and said, "Now do you want something to eat?"

Her mother managed a smile. "No, thanks, lovey. Really, I'm okay."

What her mother meant, Dana knew, was not that she was truly okay, but that she was okay without food. Her pregnancy, which had seemed endless, had been marked as much by the fact that the baby growing in her belly would never know its father, as it had by the fact that Abby had barely been able to eat a bite of food. For months she had lived mainly on soda crackers and milk, and Dana felt a pang every time she remembered privately accusing her mother of drinking at Saul's dinner party. Now she knew that her mother's illness on the ferry had been due to the baby — morning sickness, which in Abby's case had been morning, afternoon, and evening sickness.

Dana turned back to the window and at last she saw Mrs. Burger hurry by, almost running. Dana had never seen her run. Letti Burger held on to her little pink velvet hat with one hand, clutched an overnight bag with the other, and hustled up the steps to the town house.

"Mrs. Burger's here," Dana announced. "Oh, and here comes Adele, too."

"Thank goodness," said Abby, struggling to her feet. She placed one hand on the arm of the sofa and heaved herself upright, leaning backward as she did so, which always made Dana nervous.

Dana flung open the front door before Mrs. Burger had a chance to ring the bell. "The baby's coming!" she exclaimed, and flung herself into Adele's arms.

The next few minutes were a jumble of hugs and tears and questions.

"Did you call a cab?"

"Have you spoken to the doctor?"

"Where's your bag?"

"How much money do you have?"

At last a taxi arrived, and Adele helped Abby out the door, calling over her shoulder, "We'll let you know as soon as the baby is here."

Dana closed the door, turned to Mrs. Burger, and burst into tears.

Mrs. Burger gathered her to her pillowy bosom.

After a long time, Dana, still sobbing, asked, "Can I invite Patty and Marian over?"

The day seemed endless. The phone rang three times. Once it was Patty calling to say that her mother would bring her over to Dana's house at one. Once it was Marian calling to say that *her* mother would bring her over at one thirty. And once it was a man who didn't introduce himself, demanding to know just when Mrs. Burley intended to pay her very overdue and apparently very large bill. Dana handed the phone to Mrs. Burger and put her hands over her ears.

"Want to play cowboys?" Peter appeared in the entrance to the living room in quick-draw stance, ready to aim his silver pistol, if necessary.

Dana removed her hands from her ears. She forced a smile. "No, thanks. Where are Tail and Squeaky? Why don't you go play with them?"

"Yeah!" said Peter, and he loped out of the room.

Dana sank down in the chair. So many things these days could send her into a spiral of worry. The phone call from the creditor was one. So was the mention of moving. She hadn't known how quickly a person's life could change. One moment you're listening to your drunk father sing to the moon on the Staten Island Ferry, and the next your mother is telling you that your father's bank account is nearly empty.

"How is that possible?" Dana had asked when, several weeks after Zander's funeral, Abby had taken the twins out to lunch in a coffee shop and tried to explain the Burleys' shaky finances to them.

Abby had pretended to scan the menu for several moments before answering. Finally she sighed and said, "Your father was making a lot of money — a *lot* of money — but it seems he was spending it as fast as it came in. And not just on us. It turns out that he's been sending large checks to his parents in Maine."

Julia had put down her spoon and stared. "Why? Don't they have their own money?"

"They used to," their mother replied. "But your grand-dad's business failed. They moved to the smaller house, the one they're living in now, but they could only afford that because your father was helping them out."

"What will happen to them?" Dana wanted to know.

Abby had shaken her head.

"What will happen to *us*?" Julia had asked.

This was when the twins' mother first mentioned cutting back. "No more extras," she'd said. "Not until I see how much money will be coming in from your father's royalty checks. There doesn't seem to be a savings account, though, and that isn't good."

So the extras had gone first. No more spur-of-the-moment trips to Rumpelmayer's. No more evenings spent dining at the 21 Club and going to shows on Broadway. Fewer taxi rides and plenty more rides on the subway. (Peter loved the subway. "Wild West train!" he would exclaim. He insisted on wearing his cowboy boots anytime the Burleys got on the subway.)

The first phone call from a creditor had come in March. Several weeks later Abby had taken Dana and Julia aside again, only this time the discussion was held in their kitchen, where they could eat for free. Dana's mother had stared at her coffee cup for a very long time before speaking. At last she'd said, "Girls, do you understand that grown-ups sometimes make mistakes — big mistakes — but that this doesn't mean they're bad people?"

The twins had nodded their heads.

Abby paused before saying, "In your father's case, he simply wasn't thinking ahead."

"Thinking ahead about what?" Julia had asked.

"About our money. Your father was spending money he didn't have yet, certain that big checks would be coming in and that he could pay our bills then. But now he's gone and the bills keep coming in and . . . and soon there's going to be another mouth to feed."

Dana had dropped her spoon onto her plate with a *clank*. "What?"

"You're going to have a baby brother or sister. Probably in August."

Julia had jumped to her feet and hugged her mother. Dana had burst into tears and fled from the kitchen.

Now it was August and the baby was on its way. And the Burleys' house was for sale. After lunch Dana waited, alone, on the steps outside for Patty and Marian to arrive. When they did, the girls sat in a row and looked solemnly out at Eleventh Street.

"Has your aunt called yet?" asked Marian.

Dana shook her head. "Nope. No word. Mrs. Burger says sometimes it takes a while for babies to be born."

A long, dull silence followed. Dana clasped and unclasped the plastic barrette that held her ponytail in place.

"What about school?" said Patty finally.

Tears filled Dana's eyes. "I can't believe I won't be going back to Miss Fine's with you."

"But where will you go?"

"Public school. The one around the corner, I guess. Unless we leave this neighborhood when we move, and then we'll go to whatever school is nearest." Dana swiped at her eyes. "You'll probably have a new best friend by the end of the very first day of school."

"Never!" Marian proclaimed, and she took Dana's hand.

"Besides, we live right nearby. We'll still be able to see you after school."

"And on weekends," said Marian.

"I guess," Dana replied. "But you know it won't be the same."

Everything, every little thing, it seemed, was about to change. New baby, new schools (and maybe no school at all for Peter, if the public school didn't have a special class for children like him), new apartment, new everything. And now there were secrets. Dana had overheard her mother talking to Adele one night and saying that if they moved to a small apartment, they might have to give Tail and Squeaky away. She had heard her mother say that she'd need to find a job. She had heard her ask Adele whether she thought she should pack up the kids and move back to Barnegat Point. But Abby hadn't mentioned any of these things to the twins or Peter yet.

Dana and her friends continued their sad, silent vigil on the front steps. After a while, Julia joined them, plopping down next to Dana, her chin in her hands. Not long after that, Peter joined them as well.

"Stick 'em up?" he said hopefully to Julia, but she shook her head.

"I hear the phone! I hear the phone!" Dana cried ten minutes later. She got to her feet and rushed inside, followed by Peter, Julia, Marian, and Patty. "Is it Adele?" Dana asked Mrs. Burger, who was standing by the telephone table in the hallway, the phone smashed against one ear, her finger plugged into the other.

Mrs. Burger nodded. "Uh-huh," she was saying. "Uh-huh. Okay . . . Yes, of course I'll tell them. We'll see you tonight." She hung up the phone.

"Was that Adele?" Dana asked again.

"Do we have a brother or a sister?" said Julia.

Mrs. Burger gave them a sad smile. "A sister. And she's fine. So is your mother. The baby's name is Nell."

"That was our grandmother's name," said Dana. "Mom's mother."

"Hey, Peter," said Marian, "you're a big brother now!"

"Yeah," replied Peter.

"Let's go to the park," said Patty. "Could we go to the park, Mrs. Burger?"

Dana didn't wait to hear the answer. "I think I'm going to go to my room. You go on without me."

She turned away. She didn't want a baby just at that moment, thank you very much. And she didn't want to move or change schools or give Tail and Squeaky away.

She wanted her father.

As she climbed the staircase, she felt a hand slide into hers. "I'll come with you," said Peter.

Chapter 11

"Brrr!" said Dana, and drew the covers around her tightly. "It's freezing in here."

"Shh" was Julia's reply. "Let me sleep. The alarm didn't go off yet."

"I can practically see my breath."

"SHH!"

Dana peered at the clock that sat on the table between her bed and Julia's. The alarm was going to ring in two minutes. She slid out of her bed and placed a tentative hand on the radiator under the window. Stone-cold. Dana slapped the radiator. Their building's super must have thought his tenants were Eskimos. And by the way, *super* was a ridiculous name for a man who turned on the heat only when people began banging on the pipes, and who hadn't wanted to rent an apartment to Abby because he didn't like the idea of "a retard" living in the building. There was nothing super about the super at all.

Dana put on her robe and slippers and tiptoed out of the bedroom. She peeked into the next room and saw Peter slumbering in his bed, Tail and Squeaky sprawled across his feet. Jammed next to his bed was Nell's crib, where the baby slept with her bottom in the air, cozy in her flannel sleeper. In the tiny living room, Abby lay on the couch, her arm shielding her eyes from the light that shone through the window.

"When are we going to get curtains?" Julia had asked one evening, when the Burleys had been living in the apartment for nearly two months.

Her mother had shrugged and sighed. "I can't think about that right now." Abby had been sitting at the dining table, which was in the living room, since the kitchen was barely wide enough for one person to stand in at a time, let alone to accommodate a table. She'd been counting the change from her wallet, which she'd dumped onto the table.

."Don't we have enough for curtains?" Julia had asked, and in answer, Abby waved her hand toward the pitiful amount of change and glared at Julia.

"Sorry," Julia had mumbled.

Now five more months had passed and the windows in the apartment (all of them) still lacked curtains. Dana took one last look at her mother on the couch and turned back to the room she shared with her twin. The alarm rang and Julia pounded it into silence. In the next room Nell awoke and burst into tears.

Dana ducked into the bathroom, turned on the hot water faucet, held her hand under a stream of frigid water, and glared at herself in the mirror. "I hate my life," she muttered.

"Everyone out the door! March!" commanded Abby. "You're going to be late for school."

"I don't care," said Dana, but she hustled out the door anyway. Julia ran down the stairs ahead of her, Abby followed with Nell in her arms, and Peter stumped down behind all of them.

"Wait for me," he said breathlessly. He paused to glance at the door of apartment 2B, where a boy named Lawrence lived — a fifth grader in their new school who called Peter "Petard" when Abby wasn't around. Peter quickened his pace and caught up with his mother at the bottom of the stairs. "I stay home today?" he asked hopefully.

Abby gave him a small smile. "No. You have to go to school, like Dana and Julia."

"But I want my old school. I don't like this one."

Join the club, Dana wanted to say.

"Did you find your current event?" Julia asked Dana as they set out along West Eighty-Eighth Street.

Dana avoided a pigeon pecking at a bit of blueberry muffin. "I forgot."

"Miss Kent is going to kill you!"

"No, she won't. I'll say that Alaska and Hawaii have become our two newest states."

"That happened last year. You were supposed to find something from yesterday's newspaper. Miss Kent asked for a *current* event."

"How'd you get the paper anyway? We don't have one at home."

"I went to the newsstand and read one there. Miss Kent didn't say we had to bring the paper to school."

"Oh. Well, I don't have a current event and I don't care."

But Dana did care that she and Julia weren't at Miss Fine's anymore. She cared that the teachers they had known and loved since kindergarten were nearly eighty blocks away. She cared that she hadn't seen Patty and Marian since January. She also cared that Peter couldn't attend his beloved Wings Academy any longer. She did like the fact that she and Julia and Peter all went to the same school, but she cared that Peter's room was called the special class and that kids like Lawrence routinely stood outside of it and imitated the students. "Guess who I am?" she had heard Lawrence say to one of his friends the day before. He had squinted his eyes and stuck his tongue thickly out of his mouth. "Duh, I don't know what one and one is. Do you?"

His friend had burst into laughter. "Petard!" he exclaimed.

Dana turned a corner. Her new elementary school glared at her from across the street. From behind her, Abby said, "Okay, kids. I'll see you here this afternoon at two thirty sharp. Don't be late."

Dana made a face. Her mother said this every single morning, as if it were possible for Dana to forget the new family routine. Then she looked into her mother's face and saw the lines around her mouth and the purple circles under her eyes. She reminded herself that while she had to put up with Lawrence and Miss Kent, her mother had to work from three o'clock in the afternoon until eleven o'clock at night, six days a week. During the day, she took care of Nell and cooked meals and went to the market and cleaned the apartment, and then she worked at the hospital for eight hours, came home, and slept on the couch.

"We won't be," said Dana, just as Julia said, "We haven't been late once. We'll see you right here. With Peter."

Dana took Peter's hand. She led him up the steps and into Allen MacNeil Elementary School. Julia followed them. At the doorway to the special class, Julia hesitated and Dana shook her head at her, disgusted. "Never mind," she said to her twin. "You go on."

Julia scurried away.

"Okay, Peter!" Dana said brightly. "Here you go. Look, there's Mr. Thompson."

Mr. Thompson, the only male teacher at Allen MacNeil, except for the boys' gym teacher, had been hired, Dana thought, because he was big and muscular and could corral the older boys in the special class if they got out of hand.

Peter was afraid of him. And of the bigger boys.

"I stay with you?" he asked, clinging to Dana.

"Sorry. I mean, I'm *really* sorry. But I have to go to my classroom and you have to go to yours. Julia and I will pick you up at the end of the day."

"Two twenty-five," said Peter, who, if nothing else, had learned to tell time from Mr. Thompson.

Dana hugged her brother and opened the door for him. He ducked away from a fifteen-year-old boy, who had grabbed a dictionary and was hitting himself on the head with it, and took a seat at a table far from the rest of the students.

Dana slid behind her desk just as the final morning bell rang. She heaved a great sigh. Another day had begun.

Sometimes she didn't know how she would last until the end of the term. Sometimes she didn't know how she would last until the end of the day. She folded her arms across her desk and buried her face in them.

The bright spot in Dana's day was art class. One blissful forty-five-minute class with Mrs. Petrowski, who always greeted Dana with a smile and sometimes with a hug, and who allowed her to draw or paint whatever she wanted, while the other students laboriously drew bowls of pears that looked like dishes of garden slugs. Today Mrs. Petrowski hugged Dana and whispered to her, "Special treat. Why don't you go outside, sit on the school steps, and draw what you see on the street?"

This was how Dana wound up taking a pad of paper and a handful of charcoal pencils outside and sketching the things she loved about New York City. She drew a woman leaving a bakery with a bag of bread under one arm. She drew a cat sitting in an apartment window, eye to eye with a pigeon on the other side of the glass, a pigeon that seemed unmoved by the presence of the cat. She drew the sun shining on a tree that was growing on the roof of a building. When Mrs. Petrowski checked on her forty minutes later, Dana rose to her feet and bounced up the steps. "Thank you!" she exclaimed, and held out her sketches.

The moment the bell rang at the end of the day, Dana flew to Peter's class to collect him — which was easier said than done, since Peter didn't like to rush, even when he was leaving school.

"Mom's waiting," Dana reminded him over and over as he pulled on his boots, pulled on his hat, retrieved a rolled-up painting, and loped to the back of the room for a drink of water.

It was time for what Dana thought of as the switch-off. She, Julia, and Peter ran out of school, said hello to their mother, and then immediately said good-bye as Abby rushed off to her job as a receptionist at a hospital. Julia commandeered Nell's carriage and the Burley children returned to their apartment alone. Dana knew that her mother didn't like this arrangement. She also knew that her mother didn't see any other way to work things out.

"Unless we move back to Maine," Dana had overheard Abby say to Adele one evening. Adele had come over for a late-night visit. The twins and Peter and Nell had gone to bed, but Dana hadn't been able to sleep. When she heard her aunt arrive, she'd tiptoed to her bedroom door and put her ear to the crack.

"Let Pop give you some money," Adele had replied. "He's offered plenty of times."

"Absolutely not. I've paid off Zander's debts and I'm going to support the kids by myself."

"But *four* children. And in New York City. It's so expensive here."

"That's why I'm thinking about Maine."

"Pack up all the kids — Tail and Squeaky, too — and move to Maine? You don't have a job or a place to live up there. Unless you live with Pop."

"We will *not* live with Pop and Helen. Anyway, I'm not ready to leave New York yet. It's only a thought."

At that, Dana had let out a sigh of relief and returned to her bed.

Now she hefted Nell out of her carriage and struggled up the three flights of stairs to their apartment. On the fourth floor Julia was already unlocking their door with the key attached to a chain that she wore around her neck.

"Homework?" Dana asked Peter, although Mr. Thompson never assigned any to the special kids.

"You give me some," said Peter. He sat down expectantly

at the table in the living room, a composition book open before him.

Dana told Peter to write some sentences about New York City. She started her homework while Julia entertained Nell. Then Julia started her homework while Dana entertained Nell. Later, the Burleys warmed up a tuna-noodle casserole that their mother had left in the Frigidaire. After supper they watched television. They were asleep before Abby returned from the hospital.

Dana's last thought, as she lay in her bed looking through the window at the lights of a building on the other side of an air shaft, was that in eight and a half hours she would wake up and do everything all over again.

Chapter 12

Friday, September 2nd, 1960

Dana lay sweatily in the bed in the little room at the top of the beach cottage in Lewisport. Beside her, Julia sprawled across far more than her half of the bed, arms and legs flung out. Dana inched closer to the edge and finally sat up, swinging her feet to the floor. She remembered her mother saying that when she and Aunt Rose were little, they sometimes slept wrapped in each other's arms. Dana could not imagine sleeping in Julia's arms. She preferred not to touch her twin. She knew this was wrong. And yet, well, there were simply some things that certain people couldn't bear. Marian, she remembered, couldn't go near a sink if she saw a hair in it. Adele was afraid of birds — which had made walking with her along a street in Manhattan an interesting experience as Adele hopped about, avoiding pigeons that landed on the sidewalk. And Dana did not like being in such close proximity to Julia. She needed her space. But there was almost as little space here in the cottage as there had been in the apartment on Eighty-Eighth Street.

Dana sat on the edge of the bed and leaned her arms on the windowsill, looking across Blue Harbor Lane at the ocean beyond. She imagined, as she often did, her mother sitting on the bed and doing the same thing when she was a little girl and had shared the room with Rose.

Dana breathed in deeply. She smelled salt air and wet sand and dewy beach grass — all of which, she had to admit, were nicer than most Manhattan smells. She shook her head. The wet air made her hair wavy, and the breeze coming through the open window made the waves shiver.

Dana conjured up an image of the house long ago, when there weren't even screens on the windows. She used to think that seemed quaint. But now that they were living in Maine — living here for real, not just vacationing here — the cottage seemed less quaint and more shabby. It was, after all, a beach cottage, furnished with ancient beds, tables, dressers . . . and not much else.

"Where's the rest of our stuff?" Julia had asked on their first day in the house.

"It's all here," Abby said patiently.

"But — but," Julia stammered, realizing that the boxes of

clothing and books and knickknacks that surrounded them were not to be followed by any of their furniture. "You mean — this is it?"

Her mother had sighed. "There's no room for anything else. The cottage belongs to Pop and it's already full of his things. We're lucky to be able to move here. It's a fresh start."

And it's free, Dana had thought. Her mother and Papa Luther might not get along, but at least Papa Luther wouldn't charge them to live in the beach cottage.

Peter had burst into noisy tears. "What about Tail and Squeaky?"

Abby had put her arms around him. "They stayed in New York. Remember, lovey? They're city cats. They wouldn't have been happy moving to Maine."

That had been quite a lie. The cats were not in New York. They were in Connecticut with a friend of Saul's. And they hadn't moved to Maine because the Burleys couldn't afford them, not because city cats couldn't adjust to the country.

Dana slid herself carefully off the bed, dressed quietly, and tiptoed downstairs. She found her mother in the kitchen, feeding Nell.

"Hi, lovey," said Abby. "Julia up yet?"

Dana shook her head. "Is Peter still asleep, too?"

"Yes, but he and Julia will both have to get up in a few minutes. Big day."

"I suppose." It was only a big day if you were truly happy about starting over in a teensy town in Maine and having a tour of your mother's old elementary school before the fall term began.

Which Dana was not.

No matter how bad the apartment on Eighty-Eighth Street had been, no matter how bad Allen MacNeil Elementary School had been, no matter what horrible things had happened to her family in the last couple of years, Dana still preferred life in Manhattan. The cottage, Lewisport, Barnegat Point — they were all wonderful for vacation, because they were quiet and it was an adventure to get in the car and drive to the drugstore when you wanted ice cream or to the grocery store when you needed a chicken. But Dana didn't want to have to drive everywhere, even though Papa Luther had been nice enough to loan them one of his cars, in addition to the cottage. She wanted to be able to walk down the block for ice cream or chicken. And she certainly didn't want quiet. She wanted taxicabs blaring their horns and people rushing everywhere and flashing lights and crowds outside of restaurants and theatres.

Dana sat at the kitchen table and nibbled at a piece of bread.

"Could you please go wake Julia and Peter now?" her mother said. "And put on a dress, lovey. You can't go to school in dungarees."

Dana hesitated. "Mom?"

"I'm sorry, but you can't wear pants to school at any time — even just for the tour."

"It isn't that."

Abby wiped Nell's face, lifted her out of her high chair, and set her on the floor. "What, then?" she asked, her full attention on Dana.

"Did you want to come back here? I know you love New York, but you grew up in Maine, so I guess this is your home. Did you want to come back to your home?"

Abby turned and looked out the window. "New York felt like my home, too," she said finally. "If I could have made things work there, we would have stayed. But I didn't feel I had a choice about where we lived."

"Don't we always have choices?"

"No. Sometimes things just happen."

"Like when your drunk father thinks he can catch his hat by jumping off a ferry?"

"Dana!"

"Well, you were the one who was always nagging him about his drinking."

"I was not nag — Never mind. I'm not going to have this conversation with you."

Dana glared at her mother, and in an instant, Abby softened. "Maybe you think I don't know how it feels to lose a parent, but I do. I wasn't much older than you when my mother died."

"How *did* you feel?" Dana thought of the mornings when she had lain in her bed, nearly breathless with grief, and of the days at Allen MacNeil, when it had seemed as though she were separated from the other students by the loss of her father as surely as if she'd been standing behind a fence.

"Well, sad, of course."

Nell, who had been stepping around the kitchen, holding on to chair legs and Dana's legs, lost her balance then and plopped onto her bottom, her lower lip quivering.

Abby scooped her up and said to Dana, "Run along, lovey. Julia and Peter really need to get up now, or we'll be late."

Dana carried her plate to the sink and left the kitchen in silence.

*   *   *

Dana's mother parked their borrowed car on a sandy street in Barnegat Point across from a low brick building. "This is it," she said, and Dana detected a note of pride in her voice.

"What?" said Peter from the backseat.

"This is the school I went to when I was your age."

"You went to school?" said Peter.

Abby smiled. "Yes. I went to school. And I went to this very one. So did Adele and Aunt Rose. The school is bigger now, though."

"Bigger?" Dana couldn't help saying. The building was half the size of Miss Fine's and a quarter the size of Allen MacNeil.

"Much bigger. For one thing, when I went here, there was no classroom for . . . well, there was no class that Peter could have gone to. But now there's a whole new wing, with a library and an art room and extra classrooms, including Peter's."

Abby opened her door and climbed out. She lifted Nell out of the backseat, and Dana helped Peter to the sidewalk. Julia didn't move a muscle.

"Julia? Come on, lovey," said her mother. "We need to get you registered and —"

"I know. Our tour starts at ten."

"Exactly."

Julia remained in the car. "I don't want to go in. I won't know anybody."

"You know Dana," said their mother, and Dana felt an uncomfortable creeping sensation in her stomach. She didn't want to be the only person at school her sister knew.

"That's true," said Julia. She held out her hand. Dana ignored it until her sister had climbed out of the car. Then, avoiding a pointed glance from her mother, Dana finally took Julia's hand, and the Burleys walked through the entry-way to Barnegat Point Elementary School.

"I can't believe you two are going to be in seventh grade!" Abby exclaimed to the twins. "How is that possible?"

No one answered her.

Abby shifted Nell from one hip to the other. "You're getting heavy," she said. "Now let's see. If I remember correctly, the office is just around the corner."

"You're right. It *is* around the corner!" said Peter gleefully. "Look. O-F-F-I-C-E. That sign spells *office*."

"You must be the Burleys." A red-headed woman with a pleasant smile looked up from a desk by the office door. "Welcome. I'm Mrs. Harris."

"Hi, Mrs. Harris. I like this school! I do!" Peter exclaimed. "This is a nice one."

"And we're happy to have some Burleys back at BP Elementary."

Abby and Mrs. Harris chatted for a few moments, and then Mrs. Harris handed Abby several forms and a pen. "Now, you two," she started to say to Dana and Julia, but she was interrupted when three girls appeared in the doorway to the office.

"Dana and Julia Burley?" said one of the girls.

Dana instantly dropped her sister's hand. "I'm Dana," she replied.

"And I'm Julia," Julia mumbled.

"Gosh, are you really identical twins? You don't look the same. Well, not exactly the same. My name is Linda. And this is Dale and that's Susie."

"We're the seventh-grade welcoming committee," added Dale.

"Welcome!" said Susie brightly.

"Come on. We'll give you a tour."

"Great!" Dana exclaimed, stepping away from Julia.

Julia cast a helpless glance over her shoulder at her mother. "I think I'll just stay he —"

But Mrs. Harris was already guiding the twins out into

the hall with the members of the welcoming committee. "And, Peter, you'll come with me. I'm going to show you your classroom."

"Is that your brother?" Susie asked Dana.

"Yes," she replied, and nothing further was said about Peter.

"Where did you come from?" Dale asked the twins as they walked through the deserted corridors of BPES.

"New York City," Dana replied.

"New York! Gosh, I've always wanted to go there. What's it like?"

"Why did you leave it?" asked Linda.

"Yeah, and how come you moved *here*?" asked Susie.

Dana avoided Julia's eyes. She stepped a few more inches away from her. "Our mother grew up here," she said.

"Our father di —" Julia began to say.

"And she wanted a change," Dana went on loudly. "Mom thought it would be good for us. So, are there any school clubs we should know about?"

"Oh sure," Linda replied. And she and Dale and Susie told the twins about the art club, the library club, the dance committee, and the glee club. "And if you play an instrument, you can join the band. There's lots to do here."

"I'll definitely join the art club," said Dana.

"Me, too," said Julia.

Dana glared at her. "Wouldn't you be happier in the library club?"

Julia shrugged, and Dana looked away.

The tour ended, the day ended, supper ended, and just before dark, Dana slipped out of the cottage, crossed Blue Harbor Lane, and scuffed her bare feet through the cool sand. The sand by the road was as fine as flour, so she walked beside the lane for a while before turning left toward the ocean. The sand became grittier then. Cold, too, from the chilly water. Dana stopped and stood on her right leg, pressing her left foot against her warm calf, then switched feet.

Back at the cottage, her mother was putting Nell to bed. Peter would go to bed soon, too, and in a couple of hours the little house would be silent. Her mother would curl up on the couch in the living room, the very couch, she had once told Dana, on which she had sat when Zander's father, Mr. Burley, had come to tell her that her mother had died.

Dana thought about Abby. Her mother hadn't slept in a real bed since they had left the town house on Eleventh Street. Her life since then had been couches and late-night jobs and meals cooked in teensy kitchens. In a couple of weeks, as soon as Dana, Julia, and Peter were settled in at

BPES, Abby would begin another job search. Papa Luther might have provided a free house and a free car, but Abby still needed to put food on the table, and she flat out refused to take a cent from her father.

"What about Nell?" Dana had asked her mother when the subject of the job search had first come up.

"Aunt Rose will watch her while you're in school." This had been followed by a pause. "And you and Julia can watch her and Peter after school."

Dana, her feet now freezing, turned right, crossed the sand again, and began the walk along Blue Harbor Lane back to the cottage. She paused in front of a house — no lights on inside — that she knew had once belonged to her mother's friend Orrin Umhay, the one Papa Luther had never liked. Dana enjoyed hearing stories about Orrin, who (according to Abby) was bold and brave and daring and had sometimes supported his family all by himself.

The last of the daylight was fading now. Dana passed another house, a trim white cottage with blue shutters at the windows. This house had belonged to her mother's best friend, Sarah, the one who had drowned. Sarah's parents didn't live there any longer. They had moved away two years after her death, unable to live (also according to Abby) with her shadow.

Dana thought about Orrin and Sarah, about all the people

she didn't know who had once been a part of her mother's life. Her mother had lived here in this corner of Maine until she had graduated from high school — years longer than Dana had even been alive. This had been her mother's life, just as Manhattan had been Dana's life. Now Abby seemed to want this to be her children's life. But Dana belonged to Manhattan.

Dana reached the cottage and walked, now in full dark, to the front door. She let herself inside and found the living room empty. From the bedroom next to the kitchen, she could hear the low sounds of her mother reading to Peter. Grateful for the moment of quiet, Dana sank onto the couch and looked around at the treasures that had made their way from New York to Lewisport — Peter's holster and the silver gun, a copy of *Father*, Julia's postcard collection, Nell's stuffed bunny, a fairy queen doll that had belonged to Abby when she was a little girl.

Dana closed her eyes and pictured Christmas treats with her father at Rumpelmayer's, taxis that became chariots, Shirley Temples, and the water fountain in the playground and hopscotch on the sidewalk with Adele. She didn't want to start over in Lewisport. She didn't want to be the new girl or Abby Burley's daughter or Julia Burley's twin. She wanted to live in New York City and be Dana Burley, *just* Dana Burley. Loud and clear.

Outside, the breeze from the ocean became a wind, a loud wind that roared around the cottage, and suddenly Dana found herself back on the Staten Island Ferry on a frigid night in January. She felt a gust of wind come along. It snatched her father's hat and she reached out, snatched the hat back, and set it on her father's head.

Chapter 13

Tuesday, October 31st, 1961

"Bang! Bang! You're dead!"

Peter Burley, eleven years old, appeared in the doorway of the kitchen in full cowboy regalia — chaps, boots with tin spurs that spun around, a fringed vest, a ten-gallon hat, and his beloved holster and gun.

"Peter, you look great," said Dana from her place at the table.

"You'll be the best cowboy at school," added Julia.

"Where are *your* costumes?" Peter wanted to know.

"We'll bring them with us," Dana replied.

Abby emerged from her tiny bedroom. "All right, my loves. Everybody ready for school? Amy will be here in ten minutes and I don't want to be late for work."

Amy was the babysitter. The new babysitter. The Ipswich babysitter — Ipswich being not the first but the second Maine town to which Abby had moved her family after what had turned out to be a three-month stay in Lewisport. Dana and Julia had just begun to make friends at BP Elementary School when their mother said, yawning, at dinner one night, "This isn't working out."

"What isn't?" Dana had asked.

Abby had waved her hand around the kitchen and then in the direction of the living room, where her wrinkled blankets were flung about on the couch. "*This*. Any of it. I'm not making enough money at my job. I don't know how much longer I can ask Rose to look after Nell, and I certainly can't afford a babysitter. Not on *this* salary." (Abby was a part-time secretary at a lumber company.) "I've looked everywhere in Barnegat Point for a better job, but there just isn't anything. It's time to move on. Besides, we can't live in Pop's house forever."

"But it's only been three months!" Julia exclaimed.

"Have you really looked everywhere?" Dana asked.

Abby had set aside her plate of spaghetti and rested her head on her arms. "Everywhere," she'd said.

So the Burleys had packed up their things and moved to Lansdon, Maine, where Abby found a furnished apartment and where she'd sworn there were more and better jobs. She'd worked for six months as a waitress at Lobster Town, which served fried versions of everything anyone could think of, and where she'd worn a name tag that read FIRST MATE

ABIGAIL. But the money had been good and Abby had found a decent babysitter for Nell. Then Lobster Town had burned to the ground in a late-night fire and all the waitresses had swarmed Lansdon looking for other waitress jobs. After weeks of being turned down for work, Abby moved her family once again. They'd landed in Ipswich in May, when Abby had discovered that a new Lobster Town had recently been built there. She had reprised her role as First Mate Abigail.

"Well?" Dana had said to Julia on their first afternoon in Ipswich.

Julia was sitting outside on the wooden steps that led to their apartment on the second floor of an old house, chin resting in her hands. She'd sighed. "Our third school this year" was all she said.

Peter had survived each move surprisingly well. He was happy as long as he could go to school and as long as Papa Luther continued to replace the various parts of his cowboy costume as he outgrew them. The boots were the newest arrival. They'd come in a box a week earlier, along with sweaters for the twins and a snowsuit for Nell.

Now it was Halloween morning and Peter was beside himself with excitement about what the day would bring. "A parade at school, a party in my class, and tonight, trick or treating!"

"When I was a little girl," Abby said, "there was no such thing as trick or treating."

"Why not?" asked Peter.

"It hadn't been invented yet," Dana whispered to Julia.

"People didn't celebrate Halloween the way we do now," their mother replied.

"I'm going to get a whole bag full of candy tonight," said Peter. "A whole bag. Mommy, you will be home tonight to see me?"

"I will be home. Dana and Julia will take you trick-or-treating, and Nell and I will stay here and hand out candy."

"This is the best day ever!" Peter proclaimed.

At school that day Dana sat through her morning classes, doodling in her notebook and occasionally paying attention to her teachers. At lunchtime she and Julia huddled together in the cafeteria. They had an entire half table to themselves.

"Nobody even talks to us," Julia muttered to her twin.

Dana shrugged. She had given up trying to make friends at each new school. "What does it matter? We'll only be here until Mom decides to move again."

"At least she knows someone in this town, unlike in Lansdon. Maybe we won't be moving again so soon."

Dana made a face. She found her mother to be a frustrating, incomprehensible creature. Even Abby's unexpected reunion with her old friend had been puzzling. Fascinating, but puzzling. Dana vividly remembered the moment that Orrin Umhay, the subject of so many of her mother's childhood stories, had strode into their lives in Ipswich. It was during their first week there, when Abby had been working at the new Lobster Town for just three days.

At breakfast that morning she'd said, "So, kids, how would you like to have an early dinner at Lobster Town today? You could come at the end of my shift and meet my new coworkers."

"Cool!" Peter had said. "All of us can come?"

"Well, maybe not Nell. I think she should stay at home with Amy. But you and Julia and Dana could come after school. I get a discount, you know. You can order whatever you want."

"Yes! Lobster!" cried Peter, who actually did not like lobster, but liked almost every other fried item at Lobster Town.

This was how, at four thirty on a Wednesday afternoon, Dana, Julia, and Peter had happened to be sitting grandly in a row at the counter in Lobster Town, heavy white plates before them piled with French fries, fried clams, onion rings, batter-fried fish chips, fried shrimp, and fried chicken.

Their mother, in her Lobster Town uniform that made her look a little bit like a pirate and a little bit like a baby doll, had been refilling their milk-shake glasses, when Dana heard the ship's bell clang, signaling that someone had entered the restaurant. She'd glanced up from her plate and had seen a very tall, very thin, very blond policeman close the door carefully behind him and stride purposefully to the counter.

He'd chosen a seat next to Julia and spread a paper napkin in his lap.

Abby had set down the stainless steel milk-shake cup, turned to the policeman, and said, "Ahoy. Welcome to Lobster Town. I'm First Mate Abigail and I'll be . . ." Her voice trailed to a stop.

Dana had glanced at her mother. Abby and the cop were gaping at each other.

At exactly the same moment, Abby exclaimed, "Orrin?!" and the cop exclaimed, "Abby?!"

Dana stared at the man. Orrin. Orrin Umhay. The grown-up version of the little boy her mother had once played with. The boy Papa Luther had scorned because Orrin's parents were foreigners (his mother was Irish; his father wasn't actually foreign at all) and lazy (Papa Luther's opinion). The boy Papa Luther had eventually forbidden Abby to see, and whom Abby had rarely heard from after she moved to New York.

An awkward silence had followed, and then Abby dropped her tiny waitress pencil on the floor behind the counter and Orrin lost his balance and slid partway off his stool. When they'd recovered themselves, Abby had said, "What are you *do*ing here?" just as Orrin said, "What are you *do*ing here?"

Dana and Julia had raised their eyebrows at each other, and Peter had said politely, "Would you like a piece of chicken, Mr. Policeman? I didn't bite off this one yet. There's no spit."

Orrin had laughed nervously, and Dana's mother began babbling about leaving New York and moving back to Maine, while Orrin tried to explain that he now lived in Ipswich. The manager of Lobster Town, however, had shot a look at Abby and said pointedly, "You have other customers, Miss Burley." (*Miss* Burley.)

Abby had hurried to help them, her cheeks flushed, her hair escaping from the pins under her pirate hat. Orrin, meanwhile, had eaten his food in a big rush as he tried to answer a string of questions from Peter: "Can I see your gun? Do you have a holster? Does your car have a siren? Where's your police dog?"

In the end, Orrin had jumped to his feet, slid a ten-dollar bill under his plate as an enormous tip for Abby, and fled Lobster Town.

But that night he'd telephoned, and he and Dana's mother talked for two hours.

"I heard Mom on the phone with Aunt Rose last night," Julia told Dana now, leaning conspiratorially across the cafeteria table. "She said something like, 'It's good to be seeing Orrin again. He's the same as ever. Resourceful and —' And then she stopped talking and started laughing at something Aunt Rose said. So anyway I think maybe we'll be staying longer."

Dana shrugged. But she felt her cheeks start to burn and she wasn't sure why. At last she said hotly, "We'd *better* stay here." (Not that Ipswich was so great.) "Mom can't keep lugging us around like suitcases. We're actual human beings, in case she hadn't noticed."

When the last bell of the day had rung, Dana and Julia walked through Valley Road Elementary to the special classroom where they met Peter at the door. His face was sticky with orange frosting and Dana noticed frosting on the handle of his pistol and the top of one cowboy boot as well.

"We had our party!" Peter exclaimed. "It was great! And we had a parade and everyone got a ribbon. Mine says, *Great*

Costume. See? Where are your costumes? Did you have a party?"

Peter continued chattering as they walked outside, oblivious to the stares of some of the students. When Alex McDermott, an eighth grader, slapped him on the rump as he walked by and called out, "Git along, little doggie!" Peter grinned. But Dana rounded on Alex and said quietly, "I'm sure Penny will be impressed to hear how you talk to kids from the special class. I'll tell her about it tomorrow. Girlfriends find that that kind of thing *so* attractive."

"Jeez, settle down. I was only kidding," said Alex.

"No, you weren't," said Dana, and she ran to catch up with Julia and Peter. "He's such a jerk."

"Who? Alex? He's the most popular boy in our grade."

"Well, it hasn't made him any nicer."

"You know who I like?" Julia whispered as she and Dana and Peter walked across the sandy lot in front of the school.

Dana smiled. "Who?"

"Yeah, who?" said Peter.

"George Creason."

"He is cute," agreed Dana.

"Yeah, cute," said Peter.

"Who do you like, Dana?" Julia wanted to know.

Dana shrugged.

"Come on. You have to tell me. I told you."

"Okay. I like Travis."

"Travis? Travis Berman? From *Miss Fine's*?"

"Yes."

Julia said nothing.

Dana and her brother and sister skirted the edge of Ipswich and turned onto their lane. Dana looked at the weather-beaten wooden houses, one after another, that lined the street. They were tall structures, all of them white, no shutters at the windows, and they had been divided into apartments. Cheap apartments in cheap houses, thought Dana. Sticky linoleum floors, sticky Formica counters.

"Not a tree in sight," she said. "And everything is white. White sand, white road, white houses."

"I can see the ocean," said Julia tentatively, standing on her tiptoes. "It's not white."

"There's Amy and Nell!" exclaimed Peter, pointing. "Hi, Amy! Hi, Nell!"

Amy Farmer, the babysitter, sat on the bottom step of the stairs outside the apartment. She waved to Peter and the twins, and Nell waved, too, then ran to greet them. "We have cookies!" she said. "Come see."

Dana started to follow her sister up the stairs, imagining that flight of outside steps in the winter, slippery with snow.

Behind her, a horn honked and she turned around in time to see a police cruiser pull up in front of the house. "What —" she started to say.

"Yoo-hoo!" called her mother as she stepped out of the cruiser in her First Mate Abigail uniform.

The door opened on the driver's side, and Orrin Umhay unfolded himself from behind the wheel and stood looking at the house, at Amy, at Dana and her brother and sisters. Abby linked her arm through his, stood on tiptoe to kiss his cheek, and then called gaily, "Hello, everyone!"

"Hi," said Amy and Julia.

"Can I turn on the siren?" asked Peter.

Orrin smiled at him, but shook his head. "Police regulations," he replied.

Dana watched from the stairs.

"Dana?" said her mother. "Come say hi to Orrin."

Dana turned and walked up the steps, into the apartment, and through to the room she shared with Julia and Nell. She closed the door quietly. She absolutely did not want to see her mother and Mr. Umhay enter the apartment arm in arm. And she did not want to see her mother kiss Mr. Umhay on the cheek. Or anywhere else.

*　　*　　*

As soon as darkness fell that night, which was well before supper time (and well after Mr. Umhay had folded himself back into the cruiser and driven off), Peter, still in his cowboy outfit, began jumping up and down in the kitchen. "Time for trick or treating!" he cried.

Dana looked up from the table, where she was trying to write ten sentences about Ipswich in French. "Julia, could you please take him?" she said. "I think I'm going to stay here."

"But —"

"I know I said I'd go with you, but I have a lot of homework."

"Are you sure?" Abby asked Dana. "Your costume —"

Dana shook her head. Her hobo costume was okay, but she felt too old for trick or treating. "I'll stay here."

When Julia and Peter had left, and Abby had stationed herself by the top of the steps with Nell and a bowl of Hershey's Kisses, Dana slipped into her bedroom and closed the door. She reached under her mattress (the only possible hiding place in this room, which was crowded with two dressers, a pair of bunk beds, and a cot) and pulled out a packet of letters. On the upper left-hand corner of each envelope was an address on West Fifty-Third Street in New York.

Dana scrunched herself into a sitting position on the bottom bunk, selected the most recent letter from Adele, and read it for the fourth time. Then she balanced a pad of paper against her knees and stuck a pen between her teeth. She gazed out the window at the lights of Ipswich before she finally began to write.

Dear Adele,

How are you? Thank you for your letter. Things here are the same. No, that's not true. Mom has a boyfriend and I think you might know him, his name is Orrin Umhay. I'll tell you more about this in another letter.

I have to ask you something. I've been thinking about it for a long time. This is a very serious question but it's important to me, so here goes. Could I come live with you in New York? I haven't asked Mom about this yet. I wanted to ask you first, to see if it would even be possible.

I don't think I can live here anymore. I really don't. I miss you. I miss New York. Maine isn't home. I want to go home. <u>Please</u>, could I live with you? I hope you'll think about this.

Love, Dana

Chapter 14

Saturday, August 18th, 1962

"I don't understand how you could do this to us, Dana. I really don't understand."

"I'm not *doing* anything to you." Dana closed her suitcase, sat on it, and looked into the reproachful face of her twin.

"What do you mean you're not doing anything to us? You're abandoning us."

"Think of it this way. When I'm gone, you and Nell can get rid of the cot and have more space in here."

"You think this is all a joke, don't you?" Julia, disgusted, turned and left the bedroom.

"Hey!" Dana called after her. "I do *not* think this is a joke. I took it very seriously. This was a big deal and a big decision. Come back here, Julia."

"Are you fighting?" asked Nell as Julia stormed into the room. She was sitting on the cot, feet swinging back and forth. Cradled in her arms was their mother's old fairy queen doll.

"No," said Dana.

"Yes," said Julia.

Nell looked uncertainly from one twin to the other.

"Nell?" Abby called from the kitchen. "Come here for a minute and let the girls work things out for themselves."

"See, it *is* a fight," said Nell triumphantly as she exited the bedroom, holding the doll upside down by one foot.

Dana got up from the suitcase and sat on Nell's cot. "Julia," she said, "I'm really sorry you feel this way. I thought you knew how important this was to me. We've been talking about it for months."

"I know." Julia's lower lip trembled. "I guess I didn't think you would actually go through with it."

"How could you think —" Dana began to say, exasperation building in her like steam in a pressure cooker.

"It's just that I don't want you to leave," Julia rushed on. "What am I going to do without you? It was one thing when it looked like we were staying in Ipswich. But now that we're moving to Pauling, I'm going to have to start all over again at a new school — at *high* school — without you. I'll be alone. I'll spend lunchtime surrounded by empty seats."

Dana looked at the floor. "Do you want to come to New York and live with Adele and me?"

"No."

"Are you sure?"

"Yes! My family is important to me."

"Julia, it's important to me, too."

"You don't act like it is."

"Well, it is. I don't know what else to say."

"Say that you'll stay here with us."

"I can't. I'm miserable here. I hate Maine. It isn't home. New York City is home. That's just how I feel. I miss everything about it — the excitement, the skyscrapers, the museums —"

"There's a museum in Pauling."

"The fishing museum is fine, but it isn't the same as the Met, Julia, and you know it. Plus, I miss the stores and Broadway." *And I miss walking along the streets that Dad once walked along, thinking that my feet might be stepping in the exact same spots where his stepped.* "I'm just not happy here."

"So you'd rather abandon us."

"I'm not abandoning you! How many times do we have to have this conversation? I'm going back to a place I love."

"Mom feels like she failed you, you know. And Peter is really mad. That's why he hasn't said good morning to you yet."

"I — I truly don't know what to say." Dana put a trembling hand to her mouth. "We've been talking about this for so long. Mom and I have talked. Mom and Adele have talked. Adele wants me to come live with her."

"But Mom doesn't want you to go. Not really."

"Why are you telling me this today, Julia? Why didn't you tell me last week or last month? You waited until now so you could make me feel guilty."

"I did not!"

"You did, too." Dana looked at her watch. "My train leaves in an hour."

"Fine. Go get on your train."

Dana stood up. She hefted the suitcase, lugged it out of the bedroom and through the kitchen to the door at the top of the steps, and set it by her other suitcase. Every possession she owned, all stowed in two suitcases. She turned around and found herself facing her mother.

Abby gave her a small smile. "We're going to miss you, lovey."

"I'm going to miss you, too."

"I know you are."

"I won't miss you!" Peter shouted from his spot in front of the television set. Dana could hear Captain Kangaroo having a conversation with Mr. Green Jeans.

"Yes, he will," Abby whispered.

Dana nodded. "I know. And I really am going to miss all of you. It's just that I feel like I *have* to do this. New York is part of me. Plus, I'll get to go to an arts school. An *arts* school. It's a dream come true."

Abby smiled at her again. Then she clapped her hands. "Everybody into the car!" she said.

Julia's crabby voice drifted out from the back bedroom. "I'm not going."

"Yes, you are," said Abby firmly.

"No, I'm not."

Abby opened her mouth, closed it, then opened it again and said, "Peter, please turn off the television. Everybody but Julia into the car."

Peter insisted on carrying one of the heavy suitcases down the steps to the street below. Dana followed him with the other, and Abby brought up the rear with Nell. The suitcases had been stowed in the car and Dana was pulling her door closed when suddenly it was jerked open again. She looked through her window and saw Julia.

"Move over," said her twin, and slid in beside Dana and Nell. She sat silently, arms crossed, while Abby steered the car through town.

At the tiny train station outside of Ipswich, Abby bought

Dana's ticket and spoke with the porter. Dana stood on the platform with Peter and her sisters.

"I'm mad at you," Peter announced.

Julia continued to refuse to speak.

"Are you mad at me, too?" Dana asked Nell.

Nell shook her head. "Nope. I like trains."

Julia looked at her little sister in disbelief. "She's not coming back, you know."

"I am, too!" exclaimed Dana. "I'll be back at Christmas. Maybe before."

"See?" said Nell.

"You don't even know what we're talking about," muttered Julia.

"Could everyone please stop arguing?" said Abby. She handed Dana her ticket. "For heaven's sake. The train will be here in five minutes. Let's not spend Dana's last moments here in this mood."

"But I want her to stay," said Peter.

"I know you do, lovey."

Nell was the first to hear the train whistling its way around the bend before it pulled into the station. "It's coming!" she cried.

Dana hugged her family — first Peter, then Nell, then her mother, and finally Julia.

"Love you," Dana said to her twin.

Julia turned away and marched off in the direction of the car.

The porter picked up Dana's suitcases as easily as if they were empty.

"Remember," said Abby. "You change trains in Bangor and again in Boston. Find a porter to help you."

Dana nodded. She followed the porter onto the train. The moment she had taken her seat, she peered out the window and waved wildly to her family. Abby was dabbing at her eyes with a hankie but she waved back. Nell waved, too, jumping up and down, and Peter waved solemnly. The whistle blew again, the train started with a jerk, and Dana glided out of Ipswich.

The ride was long and uncomfortably warm. Dana sat by her window and fanned herself with a magazine. In Bangor, she bought a sandwich at the station. A porter helped her with her luggage and waved her on to the next train. Dana tipped him with money her mother had given her, and he said, "Good luck, little lady."

A second sticky ride followed the first one. Dana bought a Coke in Boston, and at last was on her way to New York City. As the scenery changed from rocky coastline to village to town to city, she relaxed in her seat, but when the first sky-scrapers of Manhattan appeared on the horizon, she drew in a sharp breath and sat up straight.

"Pennsylvania Station! Last stop, Pennsylvania Station! New York City!" called the conductor, making his way through the cars.

Dana felt her heartbeat quicken. The train spun along in underground darkness, emerged into a lighted labyrinth, and finally ground to a halt. Before she knew it, Dana and her suitcases were being jostled through a throng of hurrying, absorbed New Yorkers. *Home at last*, thought Dana as she struggled along.

She spotted Adele at the top of a flight of stairs and lurched toward her. They embraced for a long time.

"I missed you so much!" exclaimed Dana.

"Ditto," said Adele with a grin.

Half an hour later, Adele opened the door to her apartment with a flourish. "Home sweet home," she said.

There were the pink and blue walls, the beaded, red-shaded lamp, and the birdcage, which now housed a spider plant that trailed its vines between the bars and down toward the floor.

"That's your corner of the room," said Adele. She pointed to the daybed, which ordinarily was fixed up to look like a couch, but had now been transformed into Dana's bed. Beside it was a chest of drawers awaiting Dana's clothing and photos and trinkets. "I'm sorry you don't have a bedroom," Adele went on. "This is the best I can do."

"It's perfect," said Dana. "It's absolutely perfect. Thank you, Adele." She sat down with a sigh. "I'm going to live in New York forever."

Chapter 15

Thursday, October 25th, 1962

Dana awoke to the sound of the television. "Adele?" she mumbled, pulling her pillow over her face.

"Sorry, but I have to find out what's going on. Anyway, it's time for you to get up. You don't want to be late for school."

Dana removed the pillow and smiled. This was true. She did not want to be late. Manhattan High School for the Arts was the first school since Miss Fine's that she actually enjoyed attending. She liked everything about it — her new teachers, her new friends, her classes. At MHSA she would be able to pick a major — a major, just like in college! — and that major might be oil painting or sculpture or design.

Dana sat up in her bed and peered across the living room at the grainy black-and-white images on Adele's television set. Her aunt was standing next to the set, adjusting the antennae and squinting at the screen.

"Any changes since yesterday?" asked Dana.

"It's hard to tell. I don't think so. I wish President Kennedy would address the nation again. I feel more comfortable when I hear words coming directly from his mouth."

"I just don't think there really is going to be a nuclear war," said Dana cautiously. "Do you?"

Adele shook her head and shrugged. "Nobody thought the United States would drop an atomic bomb on anyone," she replied, "but we destroyed Hiroshima."

"And Cuba is a lot closer to the US than the US was to Japan."

"Yes. But I do have faith in President Kennedy."

"Oh, me, too," said Dana. But her stomach crawled with nervousness. The Cuban missile crisis was the scariest thing she could remember happening to her country. The Soviet Union and Cuba were conspiring to launch nuclear weapons at the United States — from Cuba itself, which was only a little over a thousand miles from New York City. "But if there *were* a nuclear war and we thought Manhattan was a target, what would we do?" asked Dana. "Would we try to leave?"

"We have a long way to go before we start worrying about that." Adele switched the television off quickly just as a newscaster intoned, "In the event of an actual nuclear war . . ."

Adele looked pointedly at the clock. "Up and at 'em," she said. "I'll start breakfast while you get dressed. Coffee and toast okay with you?"

"Yes," said Dana, who'd had her first cup of coffee the night she'd returned to New York and who now drank it several times a day, a fact she thought was better kept from her mother.

Forty minutes later, Adele locked the door of the apartment, and she and Dana started down the stairs to the ground floor, Dana carrying her portfolio, her book bag, and her purse.

"We're going to start working on self-portraits today," Dana announced. "You know what? Back when we were going to Allen MacNeil, everyone had to take art, and there was this boy in my class named Todd. And when our teacher told us we were going to paint self-portraits, Todd said, 'Who am I supposed to paint? I don't know anyone who wants their portrait painted.'"

"No!" said Adele, laughing.

"Yup. Really."

Adele held the door open for Dana and they turned left and walked to the end of the quiet, tree-lined block. Two blocks later they reached Seventh Avenue.

"It's like a different world here, and we've only come two and a half blocks," said Dana. The street was lined with office buildings, coffee shops, and hotels. Lane after lane of taxis raced by, bus gears ground, and Dana could feel the vibration of the subway below the sidewalk. Crowds of people rushed along, bumping into one another and not apologizing. Horns blared, a garbage truck wheezed past, and a man with bare feet brandished a cane as if it were a bandleader's baton while he sang loudly, "A girl fell in the toilet bowl, the toilet bowl, the toilet bowl. A girl fell in the toilet bowl. . . ."

At this, Adele grabbed Dana's elbow and pulled her along the street. "It's kind of shocking, isn't it?"

"The man?" asked Dana.

"Well, everything."

"I guess so. But I still love it. All of it."

They had reached the bus stop. "Here comes my bus," Dana said. "I'll see you tonight."

Adele thrust a bill into her niece's hand. "Can you pick up some hamburger at the market on your way home?"

"Sure." Dana kissed Adele and stepped onto the bus, juggling her possessions, and noting, before she had even paid the driver, that there were no empty seats. She shrugged and positioned herself by a man who was engrossed in his newspaper. She tried to read the front page. When her eyes fell on the words *crisis* and *nuclear*, she turned around and gazed out the window.

The crosstown bus heaved and jerked its way to the east side of Manhattan, and presently Dana jostled her way to the door and stepped into the quieter neighborhood of her new school. She had walked three blocks when she heard a call of, "Dana! Dana!"

She looked over her shoulder. Hurrying toward her, portfolio bumping against her legs, wild black hair flying around her shoulders, was Loretta Johnson.

Dana grinned. "Hi," she said, and paused to wait for Loretta to catch up with her.

"Did you do the math?" asked Loretta.

"Yes, but I don't think it's right. I'll bet you got all the answers, plus the extra credit question."

"Well . . ."

"This is an *arts* school," said Dana. "How come we still have to take math and English and history?"

"You want to be well-rounded, don't you? You *have* to be well-rounded if you want to get into college."

"I haven't thought that far ahead."

Loretta shifted her heavy book bag. "I have," she said. "Got it all mapped out. I'm going to be the first person in my family to go to college. After that I'm going to illustrate children's books."

Dana winced. Now was the moment when she should have told Loretta about *Father*, and about the fact that she'd already illustrated a book. But *Father* and the publishing parties, the days of wearing ball gowns and drinking Shirley Temples while she walked arm in arm with Zander, all seemed to be part of someone else's past. Living in the city again brought back memories, but not much more.

Dana heard another shout, and she and Loretta paused to wait for Emily Reynolds and Tanya Wen to catch up with them. (Dana was relieved that she wouldn't have to bring up *Father* after all.) They walked in a noisy group, chatting fast, interrupting one another, stopping to pull drawings out of their portfolios, until at last MHSA came into view.

The school dominated an entire block. Dana stopped in her tracks, stared at the building, and refrained from saying "pinch me" to Loretta, which she had said to her nearly every school day morning since they had first met and Dana had confessed that attending MHSA was a dream come true. It was a public school — no tuition — where Dana could study art with other kids who took it as seriously as she did, and with teachers who would encourage her as enthusiastically as Mrs. Booth and Mrs. Petrowski once had.

"Come on, girl," Loretta said to Dana. "Just say 'pinch me' and get it over with. You know you want to."

"Pinch me!" Dana cried, and she and her friends ran inside.

*   *   *

Dana's morning classes consisted of all the things she wished she didn't have to take, but knew she had to pass: English, algebra, and American history. After lunch, things improved considerably. She took classes in sculpture, painting, and commercial art, and had a private drawing lesson with a teacher named Monsieur Royale, who was inspiring but mysterious. He was an excellent teacher, who had two paintings of his own on display in the Met. If he was good enough for the Met, why was he teaching at MHSA? Dana had speculated about this with Adele one night, and Adele's response had been "Don't look a gift horse in the mouth," which Dana had taken to mean, "Don't ask too many questions."

Toward the end of the afternoon, Dana stowed her book bag in her locker and hurried toward Monsieur Royale's room. She was not twenty feet from the doorway when she heard a high-pitched siren whooping through the halls of MHSA.

"Duck and cover!" someone shouted. "Duck and cover!"

Dana's heart began to pound. She hated duck-and-cover drills. Unlike fire drills, which were sort of fun because you were pretty sure the school hadn't actually caught fire, but nevertheless you got to go outside for as long as fifteen minutes and miss, perhaps, a third of your American history class, duck-and-cover drills reminded Dana of all the things that currently terrified her. When you ducked and covered, you were protecting yourself from a nuclear blast. She imagined the flash that was supposed to come just before such an explosion. She hadn't seen one, so surely this was another drill, and not a missile fired on Manhattan from somewhere in Cuba. But still.

"All students who are in the halls, against the walls now!" called Monsieur Royale, who had rushed out of his classroom.

Dana dropped the box of charcoals she'd been carrying and leaned against a wall of lockers, forehead resting on her crossed arms. She squeezed her eyes shut. She knew that the students who were inside the classrooms had leaped out of their seats and crawled under their desks, which seemed even scarier than leaning up against a wall.

"This is just a drill, right?" Dana whispered to the boy who was standing next to her, face buried in his arms.

"I guess," he replied.

Dana held her breath and didn't let it out until the all-clear sounded.

"Go on to your classes," said Monsieur Royale.

Dana, shaking, followed him to his room, but found that she couldn't concentrate on her work.

"Settle down, Mademoiselle Burley," he said kindly.

Dana didn't settle down until school had ended and she was walking back to the bus stop in a world that seemed unchanged — taxis, garbage trucks, hurrying New Yorkers, and no bright flashes lighting the sky.

Later, back in the apartment, a meat loaf baking in the oven, Dana sat at the drawing table her aunt had managed to squish into the living room. She thought about her self-portrait. Then she thought about a new assignment — a family portrait. That was going to be interesting. Should she include her dead father in the family portrait? Should she draw just herself and Adele, since they lived five hundred miles away from the rest of her family?

Dana considered turning on the television as a distraction, but wisely decided against it. If there were more bad news, she wanted to hear it with Adele. She opened her box of charcoals and began sketching.

"Well," said Adele briskly as she and Dana were finishing dinner that evening. "I think we should call your mother tonight." Adele sounded perky, as if she were suggesting a trip to Coney Island. "We'll just check in with the Pauling crowd!"

But Dana knew that a long-distance phone call meant her aunt was worried and needed to talk to her sister.

Even so, Adele gallantly handed Dana the receiver while the phone was still ringing. "You can talk first," she said.

The phone rang once more and then a man's voice said, "Hello?"

Dana hesitated. Maybe Adele had dialed the wrong number. "Hello? Um, I'm looking for Abigail Burley. This is her daughter."

"Dana? Hello! This is Orrin Umhay. Hold on. I'll get your mother."

Dana cupped her hand over the receiver. "*Orrin* answered the phone," she hissed to Adele. When she heard her mother's voice on the line, she said, "Hi. How are you? Can I talk to Julia, please?"

"But —" Abby started to say. And then, "All right. Just a minute."

"Hello?" said Julia.

"Hi. It's me. What's Mr. Umhay doing there?"

"Orrin? He came over for dinner."

"Orrin? You call him *Orrin*? And what do you mean, he came over for dinner?"

"Just that sometimes he comes over for dinner. Pauling isn't that far from Ipswich, you know."

Dana heard Peter's voice in the background. "I want to talk to her!"

"Here's Peter," said Julia frostily.

"Dana! We're building a bomb shelter in the basement," exclaimed Peter. "In case there's a bomb. Mom bought cans of food and Orrin got us a toilet."

Dana's legs felt wobbly. She sat down heavily. "Can I talk to Mom?" she asked.

"Dana?" said her mother.

"You're putting in a *bomb* shelter?"

"Oh, I'm sure we'll never need it. Don't worry, lovey."

Dana turned panicked eyes to Adele and realized her aunt was holding out her hand for the phone. She listened to her aunt's end of the conversation until it veered from President Kennedy, Cuba, missiles, and nuclear blasts to life in Pauling and Abby's new job as a sales clerk at a clothing store.

"Want to say good-bye?" Adele whispered eventually, but Dana shook her head. She was seated at her drawing table, a sheet of paper spread in front of her, planning to draw herself, Adele, Julia, Peter, Nell, her mother, and her father, but *not* Orrin Umhay, gathered inside a basement bomb shelter.

Chapter 16

"Little Grape?" said Dana. "Are you serious? That's really the name of the town?"

Adele smiled. "That's really the name."

"Little Grape," Dana repeated. "Little Grape, Maine."

This was the conversation Dana and her aunt had the previous morning, when they had boarded a train in Pennsylvania Station in New York and Adele had handed Dana's ticket to her, saying, "Keep it safe."

Dana had examined the ticket. "How come it says *Little Grape?*"

"Because that's where the wedding will be. And where your family will live as soon as the school year is over."

My family, Dana had thought. Adele had meant Julia, Peter, Nell, her mother, and Orrin. *Were* they her family? Of course they were her family. Well, except for Orrin. Dana had met him a handful of times, but she could hardly consider him part of her family. She knew Mr. Lansky of Empire

Dry Cleaning on Fifty-Fifth Street better than she knew Orrin Umhay.

Yet Mr. Umhay was going to become her stepfather.

That very day.

In a few hours, Abigail Nichols Burley was to wed Orrin Umhay and change her name to Abigail Nichols Umhay. She would sweep her name clear of any Burley residue.

"I'm not changing *my* name," Dana had said severely to Adele the evening the news had been announced — via a long-distance phone call from Pauling on Valentine's Day.

Valentine's Day was Adele's birthday, and Dana had felt it was very callous of her mother and Orrin to mar her aunt's day with their announcement.

"No one expects you to change your name, honey," Adele had replied.

"Are Julia, Peter, and Nell going to change their names?"

"I don't know, but I don't think so. Not unless they want to."

After the Valentine's Day phone call, there had been several more calls with Abby. They were brief but mostly upbeat, both because of the wedding and because tensions had eased with Cuba, and the missile crisis was over. But Dana had sensed that her mother's excitement was curbed by something involving Papa Luther.

"Your father doesn't like Mr. Umhay, does he?" Dana had asked Adele one evening.

"Nope. Never has, as far as I know."

"But *why*?"

"Well I wasn't born yet when this happened, but apparently when your mother and Orrin were about twelve, they got into some kind of trouble and Pop forbade your mother to see Orrin again. Pop already hated Orrin, though. He'd scorned him since he was a little kid. I think he didn't like the Umhays because they're Irish — one of his parents is anyway —"

"What's that got to do with anything?" Dana had asked.

Adele had made a face. "Don't get me started on Pop and his beliefs."

"You mean his prejudices."

"Well, yes. At any rate, Pop disliked Orrin and forbade your mother to see him, and then he found out, just recently, that Orrin and your mom have been in touch off and on for years anyway."

"Wow," Dana had said, impressed.

Her mother had been keeping a secret.

Now Dana and Adele sat in the lobby of Kaylene's Motor On Inn outside of Little Grape.

"Ready?" Adele asked Dana. "You look beautiful."

Dana glanced down at her pink lace shift and the sling-back shoes that had been dyed to match the dress. "Really? Because I feel like a bottle of Pepto Bismol."

Her aunt patted her knee. "It's okay to say things like that to me, but not to your mother or Orrin, okay? This is their special day."

Dana heard the toot of a car horn and stood up. "Here they are."

"Look happy!" said Adele, and she held the door open for Dana.

Parked outside the inn, motor running, was a station wagon driven by Dana's aunt Rose. Waving from the back windows were Julia, Peter, and Nell.

"Dana! Dana! Look at me! I'm wearing a blue suit and it matches Orrin's!" cried Peter.

"I have a pink dress!" called Nell. "It matches yours and Julia's. We're samesies."

Dana climbed into the car next to Julia, who tried to slide away from her, which was impossible unless she wanted to sit in Peter's lap. Adele climbed into the front seat.

"Off we go," said Aunt Rose gaily. "Next stop, the chapel."

*   *   *

Dana had to admit that the tiny chapel at the Little Grape Community Church was pretty. The small room was painted white, the carpet running along the aisle was cherry red, and so were the cushions on the pews. On either side of the altar was a tall urn holding white snapdragons and yellow gladioli.

"We're the only ones here," Dana whispered to Julia as they stood in the doorway of the chapel.

"Mom and Orrin will be here soon. Uncle Harry's on his way with Emily, William, Lizzie, and Teddy. And Mom's aunt Betty and uncle Marshall are coming. There'll be other guests, too."

"What about Papa Luther and Helen?"

Julia shook her head. "Not coming."

"Seriously?"

Julia shrugged.

"But it's his own daughter's wedding!"

"Dana, you don't live here. You don't know what's been going on. There have been about a thousand conversations between Mom and Papa Luther. He won't come. Period. And don't bring it up. Mom doesn't want to talk about it anymore."

Dana turned at the sound of tires crunching over gravel. "There's Uncle Harry," she said.

Nell rushed out of the chapel. "Goody!" she cried. "My cousins are here." Then she turned back to Dana. "I can't amember," she said. "Are you my cousin or my sister?"

"I'm your *sister!*" Dana exclaimed.

But Nell was already running across the church lawn, calling, "Hi, Uncle Harry!"

Dana stared after her. She watched Nell fly into Harry's arms, nearly knocking him over. After that, Nell greeted each of her cousins loudly. Julia and Peter ran to the cousins, too, while Adele and Aunt Rose talked quietly.

Dana stood at the entrance to the chapel. She had the uncomfortable feeling that these people were complete strangers, that she was looking at them the way she would look at people in a filmstrip at school.

Then suddenly Nell came running back to her and tugged at her hand, crying, "Come on! Come be with us, Dana." And just like that, the spell was broken. Dana allowed herself to be led to her family and stood chatting with them until her mother and Orrin arrived.

The ceremony was short and simple and nothing at all like the one service at Papa Luther's church that the Burleys had attended when Dana was nine. They'd been visiting

Barnegat Point and Papa Luther had announced that he wanted to show off his family. In church. The Burleys were unprepared, and Dana and Julia had shown up for the service wearing pedal pushers and sleeveless blouses. Peter had been dressed in shorts and a plaid shirt with a small blue Popsicle stain on the collar.

Papa Luther had frowned at their clothes, but said nothing while Dana and Julia grasped hands before settling onto one of the hard benches. A hymn had come first, which wasn't so bad, except that Dana had never heard it before, so while Julia had struggled with the words, Dana had sung softly, "Comet, it makes your mouth turn green! Comet, it tastes like Listerine! Comet, it makes you —" That was when Papa Luther had realized what she was doing and had whacked her hands with his hymnal. Next had come a sermon so long and so scary that Dana had stuck her fingers in her ears. When she was finally released into the sticky warmth of an August Sunday, she found that nearly three hours had gone by.

"Please, may we never, ever come here again?" she had begged her father.

But the chapel in the community church was nothing like Papa Luther's church, and the wedding ceremony brought tears to Dana's eyes, even though she didn't want a new father and was fairly certain she would never think of Orrin as anything other than Mr. Umhay, the man who happened to marry her mother.

The service started at noon. The guests — there were twenty-three of them — sat close to the front of the chapel, while Dana, Peter, Julia, Nell, and Abby gathered nervously in the vestibule. When the organ began to play, Orrin stepped to the front of the chapel. At the other end of the aisle, the vestibule doors opened and first Julia, then Dana, matching Pepto Bismol girls, walked slowly down the aisle and came to a halt opposite Orrin in his blue suit, yellow hair gleaming. The doors opened again and Nell, carrying a basket of rose petals, stood uncertainly at the end of the aisle. Behind her, Abby gave her shoulder a gentle nudge, and suddenly Nell sprinted down the aisle to her sisters, tossing the entire basket to Adele as she flew by. The laughter was just subsiding when the doors opened for a third time, and Peter and his mother, arm in arm, began the walk to the front of the chapel. Nell was disappointed that her mother didn't look like a "real bride," with a veil over her face and a white train trailing behind her, but Dana (secretly) approved of Abby's beige suit. At the altar, Peter, smiling and very calm, gave

Abby a kiss on the cheek, unlinked his arm from hers, handed her to Orrin, and sat down next to Adele, all as rehearsed the evening before. (This was the first time Dana's eyes filled.)

The minister spoke briefly about marriage and what it means, and then the vows were exchanged, Orrin kissed Abby lightly, and Nell covered her eyes and said, "Ew!" at the top of her lungs. For some reason, this was the second time that Dana felt herself go teary.

Later everyone stood outside the church holding handfuls of rice and waiting for the bride and groom to appear.

"There they are! There they are!" shrieked Nell. She was the first to toss her rice at Abby and Orrin, and it landed ten feet in front of them. "That should do it," she said, dusting her hands off.

The reception was held in the fellowship room at the church — the bride, groom, and guests circling around to the back entrance and climbing a flight of stairs, following the smell of coffee and pastries.

Dana lost track of Adele and stood uncertainly by herself for several moments. Then she poured a cup of coffee and began to circle the room in search of Peter.

"What do you think you're doing?" A hand gripped her elbow.

"Julia? I'm looking for Peter. What's the matter?"

Julia pointed to the cup in Dana's hand. "That will stunt your growth, you know."

"Oh, it will not. That's an old wives' tale. Anyway, how much more do I need to grow?"

Julia shrugged.

"So," said Dana. "We never really get to talk. How was school this year?"

"The same as when you asked me in December."

"Do you have to go to a new school in the fall?"

Julia made a face at her. "Duh. Unless I want to travel thirty miles to Pauling every day."

"How come you're moving again anyway?"

"Because," said Julia, sighing loudly as if she were talking to a two-year-old, "Orrin quit the police force and he's opening his own automobile repair shop here. Plus, he found a nice house for us in Little Grape. There's no reason for him to travel back and forth from —"

"Okay, okay. Jeez, Julia, I'm just trying to make conversation."

"Then you could at least have stayed with us last night instead of in the motel with Adele. We would have had plenty of time to talk."

"But Mom said there wasn't enough room at the house! She said Aunt Betty and Uncle Marshall were staying with you."

Julia shrugged again.

"Besides, if you wanted me to stay with you so badly, you could have asked me. I'm not a mind reader."

"You're my *twin*. I shouldn't *have* to ask you stuff like that."

Dana sighed loudly. "Well, I'm here now. And I'm trying to talk to you."

Julia looked at her watch. "You'll have to talk fast. The reception ends in an hour."

"There are my girls!" boomed a voice, and Uncle Marshall appeared between the twins. "So, how is life in the Big Apple, Dana? Is it good to be back?"

Dana smiled. She began to describe her classes at MHSA. She was draining her coffee when she realized that Julia was no longer there.

That evening, tired, their feet aching, Dana and Adele fell into their beds at Kaylene's Motor On Inn.

"Did you have fun?" Adele asked sleepily.

Dana hesitated, and then burst into tears.

"What's the matter?" said Adele, alarmed.

"I don't fit in here anymore. It's like I'm not part of my own family."

Adele slid out of her bed and drew Dana into her arms. "Do you want to stay here, then?"

A fresh sob. "No! I can't wait to get back to New York."

Dana kissed her aunt good night and turned out the light.

Chapter 17

Friday, November 22nd, 1963

"Dana." Her aunt shook her shoulder.

"Five more minutes," mumbled Dana.

"I gave you five more minutes ten minutes ago. And ten minutes before that."

Dana wrestled herself to a sitting position. "Really? What time is it? I don't want to be late."

"It's seven o'clock."

"Seven!" Dana shot out of bed, grabbed a handful of clothes out of her dresser, and made a dash for the bathroom.

"Are you going to have time for breakfast?" Adele called through the closed bathroom door.

"No."

"You can eat a bagel on the way to school, then."

"That's okay. I have lunch at ten forty-five, remember?"

This was true. When Dana and her guidance counselor had worked out Dana's schedule of classes for her sophomore year at MHSA, the counselor, Mr. Radnor, had looked up cheerfully from his desk and said to her, "Well, you're going to be busy. It looks like the only period you'll have free for lunch is fourth. Ten forty-five. Okay?"

Dana had shrugged. What choice did she have? Besides, she might come home from school starving every day, but she felt that was a small price to pay in exchange for being able to take photography and architecture.

"Did you stay up too late?" asked Adele when Dana eventually emerged from the bathroom.

She shook her head. "I just couldn't sleep."

"Anything wrong?"

"Not really. I was thinking about our phone call last night. It was nice to talk to Mom and everyone, instead of reading letters, but it was weird, too. It's funny to think of them in Little Grape — a family with a dad — and I'm not really part of it. Nell doesn't even know me anymore. She wouldn't talk to me."

"She's only four, honey."

"I know, but she used to want to get on the phone and say hi. Now she acts like Mom is asking her to talk to Helen."

Adele watched Dana gather her books. "You can always change your mind, you know. You can always go back."

Dana shook her head. "No. I can't. I wouldn't be happy there. And I am definitely happy here." She gave her aunt a hug. "Let's go. Today's important. I have to give a report in first period. And last period is — sigh, gasp — life drawing with Mr. Friedman."

Adele frowned. "You have a crush on Mr. Friedman?"

"No! On Randall Goodman. He sits next to me in life drawing."

Adele's frown was replaced with a grin. She opened the door. "Off we go," she said. "Another day."

And that was how November 22nd, 1963, began. Dana and Adele hurried to Seventh Avenue. Adele's bus arrived first and she called over her shoulder, "Stop at the market on your way home!" before she boarded.

Dana's bus chuffed along a few minutes later and she struggled up the steps with her belongings and actually managed to find a seat. She pulled off her gloves and blew on her cold fingers, while mentally rehearsing the report she'd had to memorize for first period.

The report went fine and the morning went fine. Dana was starving by ten forty-five and ate her lunch so fast that Loretta, who had also gotten stuck in fourth-period lunch, said, "Slow down, Hoover." Dana did slow down, but by the last period of the day, she was famished again. She was so hungry, in fact, that she decided she needed to tell a little lie to Mr. Friedman. Not a lie, she corrected herself as she hurried through the corridors a few moments later; she had just needed to misdirect him. So she'd asked for a pass to the bathroom, but instead had run to the lunchroom, where she'd bought a bag of potato chips just as the cafeteria was closing for the day. She was on her way back to Mr. Friedman's room, Hoovering down the chips, when she heard the buzz that meant an announcement was about to come over the PA system.

"All students report immediately to their homerooms," said the hollow voice of Mrs. Parson, the principal. "Repeat, all students report immediately to their homerooms."

Dana's heart began to pound. She had never heard such an announcement. Report to their homerooms? Now? At the end of the day, with just a few minutes left in the final period? Mrs. Parson had sounded very grave. Maybe a little panicky, Dana thought.

She quickened her pace. The halls had been mostly empty, but now doors began to open and students poured out of the classrooms.

"What is it?" Dana asked somebody.

"Don't know."

Dana threw the remainder of the potato chips into a trash can and made a dash for Mr. Friedman's room. Her classmates were already leaving. Dana grabbed her things from her desk. "What's —" she started to ask her teacher, but he was talking to Miss Rafferty from the adjoining room, and Dana thought — was it possible? — that both of them were crying a little.

She flew back into the hall and up the stairs to her homeroom. The chatter around her was alarming. "National tragedy," she heard someone say. "Emergency." "Disaster." One girl burst into tears and gripped the arm of her boyfriend. "Is it a nuclear war?" the girl asked him. "Are we supposed to duck and cover?"

Dana slid behind her desk, the last one to reach her homeroom. Tanya Wen was sitting in front of her. She tapped Tanya's shoulder. "What happened?" she asked.

Tanya turned around and Dana saw that her lip was quivering. "I heard something terrible."

"What? What did you hear?"

"I heard that President Ken —"

"May I have your attention, please?" Mrs. Antonelli, who was Dana's homeroom teacher as well as her English teacher, clapped her hands, and the class immediately became quiet. Tanya faced front again. "I'm afraid I have some very bad news," Mrs. Antonelli began. "There's no easy way to say this. We've just heard — and we don't have many details yet — that President Kennedy has been shot."

Dana gasped. In front of her, Tanya's shoulders shook.

"Is he going to be okay?" someone asked.

Mrs. Antonelli stared out the window. "No," she said. "He's been assassinated. He died just a little while ago." She pulled a handkerchief from her pocket and held it to her eyes.

Later — years later, decades later — Dana would recall all sort of things about the rest of this day. She would remember Tanya's shaking shoulders and Mrs. Parson's panicky voice on the PA system and news broadcasts and the look of devastation on Loretta's face when they met at their lockers a few minutes later. But whenever anyone asked her what she remembered about the day President Kennedy was shot, the first thing she always said was, "My teachers were crying." She had never seen her teachers cry. Well, once, in English class, when Monty Biggs, who was pimply and being raised by his grandmother, had read a poem he'd written about an orphaned chicken, she had seen Mrs. Antonelli's student teacher tear up, but Dana felt that hardly counted. It was nothing like today.

Today. November 22nd, 1963.

Dana knew, almost the instant she heard Mrs. Antonelli say, "He's been assassinated," that those words drew a before-and-after line in America's history, in the same way that the moment her father had reached for his hat on the ferry had created a before-and-after line in her own history.

Mrs. Antonelli was now so choked up that when Tanya timidly raised her hand and asked, "What happens to our country now?" she could only shake her head.

For a few moments the room was as still as Manhattan in the soft haze of a snowfall. Then the boy next to Dana said angrily, "Who shot him?"

Mrs. Antonelli reached for a tissue and blew her nose. "I don't know. There really isn't much information yet."

"What *does* happen to our country now?" Tanya asked, this time more forcefully.

"The vice president —"

The door to the room opened then and a teacher Dana didn't know stuck her head inside. "What are we supposed to be doing?" she whispered loudly. "The bell is going to ring soon."

"I haven't heard anything," Mrs. Antonelli replied. "I don't know. I guess we just sit tight."

Dana closed her eyes. She tried to imagine someone evil enough to kill President Kennedy. To *kill* him. Almost everybody Dana knew loved the president. She remembered the night in Maine when her family had heard the news that John Fitzgerald Kennedy had been elected the thirty-fourth president of the United States of America. It had been one of the bright spots in that autumn of adjustments and disappointments. Papa Luther had not voted for Mr. Kennedy, of course, but Dana's mother had, and when the news came over the radio, she had laughed — actually clapping her hands while she did so — and then burst into happy tears.

Now Mr. Kennedy was dead. And he hadn't died naturally, he'd been killed. Murdered.

Dana heard the buzz of the intercom and jerked to attention. "Everyone is dismissed," Mrs. Parson said quietly. "You may all go home."

An early dismissal, even one that was only a few minutes early, generally caused great cheering and jumping out of seats, chairs being knocked over backward. But when the intercom went quiet, Dana's classmates got to their feet wordlessly and filed into the hall. The halls, too, were quiet, filled with dazed students and dazed teachers.

Dana gave Tanya's hand a squeeze and said, "I'll call you over the weekend." She met Loretta at their side-by-side lockers. "Want to come over?" she asked.

Loretta shook her head. "I have to find Ma. I hope they let her off work. She'll want to go to church."

"Can't you go to church tomorrow — or Sunday?"

Loretta stared at her. "This is President Kennedy we're talking about. President *Kennedy*. We have to pray for him."

Dana left school alone. She walked to the bus stop, saw her bus coming, ignored it, and continued walking. All around her were stunned faces. Women hugged one another on the street. Men cried. People streamed into churches.

Dana walked. And walked and walked. She walked until at last she was standing in front of the building that housed Bobbie Palombo's costume shop. Dana had been to the shop before, of course. She'd been there many times. But never unannounced. Now she walked through the lobby to the elevator bank, pressed the brass button, and rode the elevator to the sixth floor. She turned left, then left again, and reached the wooden door with the frosted-glass window and the black letters (peeling slightly) that read simply BOBBIE PALOMBO. She knocked twice and entered.

Inside she found Adele, Bobbie, and two other women huddled around a radio. Half-finished costumes had been abandoned, and the other workers had apparently already gone home. Adele rose when she saw Dana. "Honey," she said, arms open.

Bobbie flicked her hand toward the door. "Go, go," she said, her voice catching.

"I walked here," Dana told her aunt as they rode the elevator back to the street. It was the only thing she could think to say.

They edged around a crowd of people gathered outside an appliance store, watching a television through the window. The owner of the store had turned up the volume so that the newscaster's voice could be heard on the street.

The president was dead.

He had been shot in Dallas.

His beautiful wife had been covered with her husband's blood.

"Nothing will ever be the same again," said Adele.

Chapter 18

It had been a long time since Dana had awoken in the beach cottage on Blue Harbor Lane. But now here she was, lying in a sleeping bag between Julia and Nell. Three army-green sleeping bags in a row on the floor, Peter splayed across the couch on the other side of the room, one bare foot sticking out from beneath a blue-and-white afghan that Aunt Rose had crocheted.

Dana turned over and found herself facing the wide brown eyes of five-year-old Nell.

"I stared you awake," Nell whispered. "That's how you wake someone up without making a sound. You just stare."

Dana had been awake for nearly half an hour while her brother and sisters slept soundly around her, but she said, "That's pretty smart."

"I am a smart person," Nell agreed. "Very smart. Did you know that I will be in first grade this fall?"

Dana knew. Of course she knew. Nell was her sister.

"You live in New York City, right?" said Nell.

"Yup."

"And what do you do in New York?"

"Well, I go to school —"

"Have you been to the Empire State Building?"

"Yes."

"To the tippy top?"

"Yes."

"Hmm. Sometime maybe we can visit you there. Sometime — Hey, look. Peter's awake — and I wasn't even staring at him."

"I'm awake, too," said Julia, yawning.

"Let's all take a walk on the beach," said Dana. "Before the grown-ups get up."

The four Burleys were on their feet in a flash. They threw on their clothes and winter coats.

"Can we go barefoot?" asked Peter.

"Nope," said Julia firmly. "It's only April. Way too cold. Wear your sneakers. We can walk along the sand, but not in the water."

Dana looped her elbow through Peter's as they crossed Blue Harbor Lane. "Look how tall you are," she said. "Almost as tall as me."

Peter grinned at her. "I'm fourteen. That's a teenager."

It had been Orrin's idea to spend spring break at the cottage. "Wouldn't it be fun?" Abby had said when she'd phoned Adele and Dana one night in March. "A family vacation. All of us at the cottage. Orrin suggested it."

Somehow it had worked out. Dana's school vacation had coincided with Little Grape's spring break. Adele had asked Bobbie Palombo for a week off from work. Orrin had arranged for two of the mechanics from his auto repair shop to run the business while he was away. Abby had begun packing and planning.

Dana had been eager for the vacation to start. She missed her family. And she had to admit that, like him or not, Orrin seemed . . . good. When Dana had visited Little Grape at Christmastime, she'd found a mother who no longer had to arrange for endless babysitters and who could sit at the table and enjoy breakfast with her family. She'd found a twin who laughed easily and who, at last, had made friends of her own. Peter and Nell called Orrin Dad, which had startled Dana, but she'd said nothing about it. After the phone call from her mother, she'd begun counting the days until April 10th, when she and Adele would take the train north to Maine.

Then four days before the official start of spring vacation, Mr. Radnor had sent a note to Dana, asking her to schedule an appointment with him.

"This can't be good," Dana had said ruefully to Loretta. She'd held the note out to her friend. "When is a note from your guidance counselor ever good?"

"You never know," Loretta replied dubiously.

Dana had scheduled the appointment for the next afternoon and had waited in the orange plastic chair outside Mr. Radnor's office, jiggling her foot and biting her nails.

When the door to his office had opened, she jumped.

"Dana," Mr. Radnor said warmly. "Come in."

Dana perched on the edge of the chair opposite his desk and looked at the photos tacked to his bulletin board. Mr. Radnor and a dark-haired woman sitting side by side on a sofa, smiling self-consciously. Three pigtailed little girls in identical two-piece bathing suits, holding up red sand shovels. A sheepish-looking cocker spaniel wearing a necktie.

Mr. Radnor pulled a sheet of paper out of a folder. "I have good news for you," he said, and Dana felt herself go limp with relief.

"You do?" she said weakly.

"Yes. Excellent news, as a matter of fact. Have you heard of the Prescott School of Design in Massachusetts?"

"Sure," Dana replied. "It's one of the best art and design colleges in the country."

"What would you say if I told you that they've invited you to apply for a scholarship?"

Dana had hesitated. "Is that good? I mean, I was going to apply to Prescott next year anyway."

Mr. Radnor smiled at her. "It's very good. When Prescott *invites* you to apply, it means they already want you. And the invitation almost *guarantees* you a scholarship. A full scholarship."

"You're — are you serious?"

"Absolutely. This is quite an honor, Dana."

"I can't believe it. I've been dying to go to Prescott, but I didn't know how I was going to afford the tuition. I have a twin sister and she wants to go to college, too, and there just isn't enough money. I was going to ask you about scholarships next year."

"I think you can relax a little, then. I mean, if Prescott is where you'd like to —"

"Oh, it is!"

"All right. You still have to go through the application process and get your portfolio together. And of course you have to keep up your grades, which are excellent. But if you can do those things, then I think you'll be going to Prescott on a full scholarship."

Dana had left the office feeling dazed, and had immediately run into Loretta, whom she suspected had been waiting for her.

"Girl?" Loretta had said.

Dana burst into tears. "I'm going to Prescott."

Somehow Dana had managed to keep this news a secret. Four days had passed since her meeting with Mr. Radnor, and Loretta was the only person Dana had shared her news with. She felt a little guilty about her windfall. Loretta needed a scholarship just as much as Dana did. There were only two kids in Loretta's family, but her parents earned less money than Orrin.

"I'll bet Prescott gives out lots of scholarships," Dana had said, although she had absolutely no idea how many scholarships Prescott offered each year.

"Sure," Loretta replied. "But anyway, I'm applying to Rizzdee."

"What?"

"Rhode Island School of Design. RISD. Everyone just says *Rizzdee*."

That was the last either one of them had said about scholarships before they'd parted ways for spring break.

On Saturday, Dana and Adele had boarded the train for

Maine and somehow, during the long hours of that endless ride, Dana said not one word about Prescott. She thought about it constantly, though. While Adele read and worked crossword puzzles and drew designs for a flapper costume, Dana thought about going to college and about whatever would come after that.

Prescott was her dream. She planned to soak up everything she could while she was there and then embark on a career as an illustrator. Or maybe a designer. But probably an illustrator. In any case, she wanted a career. Her mother could have had a career. Papa Luther hadn't let her go to college, but that didn't mean anything. After all, Adele hadn't been allowed to go to college either, and she had a career. Dana's mother was a good writer. She could have been a writer like Zander. Or maybe she could have worked for a magazine or for a book publishing company. Something. But she had gotten married and stopped writing and started having kids, and when Zander died, she'd had no way to support them.

Dana was not going to let that happen to her. She had a firm plan: go to Prescott, establish a career in the art world — a good career that would pay lots of money — and later get married and have a baby. Maybe. But she did not plan to find herself in the position in which her mother had found herself after Zander had died, toting her children from place to place, counting out change from the bottom of her pocketbook.

Now, as Dana tromped along the beach with her sisters and brother, the words *Guess what — I'm going to Prescott* were on her lips. "Guess —" she started to say. She felt Julia's hand on her elbow and looked into her twin's smiling face. Ahead of them, Peter was loping across the sand, calling, "Bet you can't catch me, Nell," and Nell ran after him, but not, Dana noted, at her top speed.

"What?" Dana said to Julia.

"Nothing. This is just . . . nice."

"Yeah."

"So how is everything in New York?"

"Great. I still love my school."

"Me, too. I mean, mine isn't a special school like yours, but I really like it."

"I'm glad."

"How's Loretta?"

"She's fine."

"She's the one who's black?"

Dana frowned and Julia blushed.

"Sorry. Don't worry," Julia rushed on. "I'm not turning into Papa Luther. I'm just trying to keep your friends straight.

I have a best friend now, too." She hesitated. "You don't mind, do you, Dana?"

"Of course I don't mind!"

"And," said Julia, lowering her voice to a whisper, "I have a boyfriend."

"Really? That's great." Dana thought Randall Goodman and a few other guys at school were cute, but the last thing she wanted was an actual boyfriend. She could see that Julia was happy, though.

"His name is Royce."

"Is he cute?"

"He's the cutest boy in our whole grade. He's taking me to a dance in a few weeks. But that's a secret for now, okay? I don't feel like telling Mom yet."

"Okay."

Dana waited until her family was assembled for breakfast that morning and then, at last, she divulged her own secret. "I've known this for a few days, but I wanted to tell you when we were all together." She glanced at Adele. "Boy, was it hard to wait." Adele smiled at her. "I have really good news. Prescott invited me to apply for a scholarship. My guidance counselor said that means I'm practically guaranteed one."

"Prescott?" asked Orrin.

"It's a college for art and design," Dana told him. "It's an honor to be asked to apply."

"Lovey, that's wonderful!" Abby leaped up from the table and put her arms around Dana.

"The best thing," Dana continued, "is that it's a full scholarship. So, Julia — maybe you'll get a scholarship to college, too, but if you don't, well, this should make things easier."

Orrin smiled at Dana from across the table. "We're proud of you. Awfully proud. You've worked hard."

"I'll say she has," said Adele.

Dana turned to her twin.

"I'm really happy for you," said Julia.

A week later Dana and Adele stood on the platform at the train station. In a knot around them were Abby, Orrin, Julia, Peter, and Nell. When the train whistle sounded in the distance, Nell shouted, "Here it comes!" and Julia drew Dana away from the family.

"I'm going to miss you," she said.

"Me, too."

"This was the best vacation ever."

"Let's write more often," said Dana.

"Definitely."

Chapter 19

Wednesday, August 3rd, 1966

Dana sat alone at the scarred table in the kitchen of the house in Little Grape. Only five thirty in the morning, but she was wide awake. The house was too still. She longed for all the noises of the apartment in New York, the noises that lulled her to sleep in a way that no amount of Maine quiet could.

She stood up, considered making a cup of tea, then sat down again, and was still sitting in the uncomfortable wooden chair, doing absolutely nothing when her mother shuffled into the room and sat across from her. Abby's eyes were puffy and her hair was rumpled from sleep. She was wearing a fuzzy blue bathrobe that Dana was certain was at least eight years old.

Dana tried to see the mother she'd known long ago in New York. The mother who had arranged birthday parties and worn long gowns to balls and dined at the fanciest restaurants in the city. She didn't see that mother. She saw a woman who looked old, although she wasn't really, whose hair was shot through with gray, and whose hands showed signs of hard work and hot dishwater.

Abby tried to smile. "What are we doing up at this hour? We got such good news yesterday. Better than we'd hoped for. We should be sleeping like babies."

Dana didn't answer. She thought back to the previous Saturday. Just four days earlier. It seemed as though her summer had spun out of control in those four days. Before Saturday, her summer had drifted along in a lovely, predictable routine. She'd spent her days working alongside Adele at Bobbie Palombo's, a job that was interesting and paid nicely. Dana had saved almost all of her earnings, and felt they would cover the few things her scholarship to Prescott wouldn't cover — train fare to Manhattan or Maine on holidays, spending money, art supplies. She'd been working at Bobbie's ever since her graduation from MHSA in June.

Dana's graduation had been wonderful. Her mother, Orrin, Julia, Peter, and Nell had taken the train to Manhattan and stayed for three days (her mother and Orrin in a hotel, her sisters and Peter camping out on Adele's floor), and cheered Dana on as she'd graduated from high school with honors. They'd visited the Statue of Liberty and had gone to the tippy top of the Empire State Building, which Nell had enjoyed, although she'd been disappointed not to see a single sign of King Kong. "Not even a bit of his fur!" she'd wailed.

At the end of their visit, Adele and Dana had traveled back to Maine with them and cheered Julia on as she'd graduated from Ronald Casey Central High School, also with honors, bound for Bates College in Lewiston, Maine, in September.

And then . . . Saturday morning.

A Saturday morning in New York City in August. Dana and Adele had slept late, eaten breakfast late, and were finally getting ready to leave the apartment.

"Do you really have to go into work?" Dana had asked her aunt.

"I really do. Just for a few hours. Bobbie needs me. I'll be done by two. Three at the latest."

"Okay. I'm waiting for Loretta to call. She and Tanya and I are going to Gimbels."

Adele had smiled. "More clothes?"

"Nope, just lipstick. For me anyway. Pink frosted. I don't want to spend too much."

Dana, Loretta, and Tanya were tight with their money, a fact that amused Adele. All three girls had been awarded scholarships to art colleges, all were very grateful, and all were extremely careful where their finances were concerned.

"You're like a bunch of old ladies!" Adele had exclaimed once, and Dana had taken this as a compliment. She had her dreams and she had her plans. They all centered on being an artist — and being self-sufficient.

And then the phone had rung.

"That's probably Loretta," Dana said. She kissed her aunt on the cheek. "See you this afternoon." She picked up the phone as Adele stepped into the hallway. "Hi!" Dana said. "Are you ready? I'm — What? Mom? . . . Oh — Adele! Wait! Come back!"

Adele had turned around, a question mark on her face. Dana, already trembling, thrust the phone toward her aunt. "It's Mom," she whispered. "She said that Julia . . . Just talk to her."

Dana had sat on the floor, arms wrapped around her knees, and listened to Adele's end of the conversation. She was only two feet from her aunt, but had felt as if she were seeing her through a tunnel — a tiny, faraway figure. She caught a word here and there. *Meningitis. Hospital. Train.* The conversation was brief. It had ended with Adele saying, "We'll be there as soon as we can. I'll let you know what train we'll be on." She looked down at Dana. "Do you want to talk to your mother again?"

Dana had hesitated, then held out her hand for the phone. "Mom? What *is* meningitis? How did Julia get it?"

Abby had tried to explain. Dana listened to the hurried description of an inflammation of the membranes surrounding the brain and of Julia's symptoms — her stiff neck, the fever.

"Is she going to die?" Dana had finally whispered.

There was a pause at the other end of the phone. "The doctors don't know. It's very serious."

Dana had said nothing. She held the phone out to Adele.

After a few more murmured words, Adele had said, "All right. We'll be in touch," and she hung up.

Dana suddenly exclaimed, "Loretta! I was waiting for her to call. We're supposed to go shopping! And you're supposed to go to Bobbie's."

"Settle down," Adele had said gently. "Let me make some phone calls."

Dana had let her aunt do everything, including phone Loretta to tell her what had happened. Somehow the day passed, Dana still seeing the world through the tunnel. By late in the afternoon, they were boarding a train north. Dana had sat nestled against Adele, her head on her shoulder, unaware of the curious glances of the other passengers. It was well after midnight when they'd stepped off the train and looked up and down the platform for a familiar face.

"Who's going to meet us?" Dana had asked.

"I'm not sure."

A few seconds later Aunt Rose had wrapped them in her arms and led them through the silent Maine night to her station wagon.

Sunday and Monday had passed slowly, the events viewed again through Dana's tunnel. Dana and Adele took turns joining Abby and Orrin at Julia's bedside. When Adele was at the hospital, Dana stayed at home with Peter and Nell, fielding their constant questions.

Is Julia lonely at the hospital? (Peter.)

Am I going to catch her benavitis germs? (Nell.)

When is she going to come home? (Peter.)

How do you get benavitis? (Nell.)

When is she going to come home? (Peter, the question asked endlessly.)

When Adele stayed at home, Dana went to the hospital. The first time she saw her sister, her breath had caught sharply in her throat. Julia was the sole patient in a two-bed room, the other bed rumpled because Abby had slept in it the past few nights. Julia had been asleep when Dana entered the room, but had slowly woken and offered her sister a wan smile before drifting off again. She had looked pale and tiny, and Dana had understood why the doctors wouldn't say for sure whether her sister would make a complete recovery. There was talk of brain damage and hearing loss.

Then on Tuesday afternoon, Dana had entered the room, now overflowing with balloons, flowers, and get-well cards, and found Julia propped up in her bed, her cheeks looking as if someone had brushed them lightly with pink watercolor.

Julia brightened. "Dana. What are you doing here?"

"I've been here since Saturday night."

"Really?"

Dana sat gingerly on the edge of the bed. "Is it okay to do this? Am I hurting you?"

Julia had smiled and shaken her head. "You're not hurting me."

"Mom?" Dana said. "Orrin? Why don't you go down to the cafeteria? You've been here all morning. Julia and I will be fine."

"I guess we could use some coffee," Abby replied.

When Dana and her sister were alone, Dana said, grinning, "Well, you really did it this time."

Julia smiled back. "Wow. I can't believe how bad I felt. I mean, before I went to the hospital. My head, my neck . . . How long did you say you've been here?"

Dana had told her sister about Saturday — about the phone call and the train ride to Maine. "Nell thinks you have something called benavitis," she added. "And Peter just wants to know when you're coming home."

"I had such a weird dream," Julia said suddenly. "I just remembered it. There was this empty room, and you and I were the only people in it. We were standing against opposite walls, and even though the room wasn't very big, it was like we were really far apart. And I kept calling you but you couldn't hear me." She paused. "Maybe that's why I'm surprised to see you."

Dana had laughed. "I guess you don't have to be an expert to figure that dream out."

"What?"

"It's obvious. We learned all about dreams in this psychology class I took last semester. Dreams are fun to analyze." Dana had inched closer to her sister. "Julia, I know you think I deserted you when I decided to live with Adele, but I really didn't. I mean, maybe it felt that way to you, but I just couldn't stay here any longer. I was going crazy moving around Maine. You didn't know how much I missed New York."

"Yes, I did. I knew. I just didn't want you to leave. I guess that was selfish."

"No, it wasn't. We want what we want. But I hope you truly know that I didn't leave because I wanted to leave you and Mom and Peter and Nell. I love all of you. It was just that I had to go back to New York. I *had* to. New York was where we had lived with Dad. It was where I'd been happy. Maybe that was selfish of *me*."

"No." Julia had reached for a cup of water and taken a sip. "It's like you said. We want what we want. We each wanted different things."

"But we still love each other. I loved you then and I love you now."

Julia's eyes had filled. "Of course we love each other."

Dana had reached for her twin's hand then and held it until her mother and Orrin returned.

Now Dana and Abby were seated across the table from each other.

"It *was* the best news," Dana agreed. "The best news the doctors could have given us." Three doctors had entered Julia's room the previous afternoon to proclaim that Julia was out of the woods. "Not even any permanent damage," Dana went on.

"She'll have to postpone college, though," said Abby.

"Just for one semester. That's not so bad."

Abby shook her head. "And off you go again."

"What?"

"You said that so easily. 'Just for one semester.' In a few weeks you'll be leaving for Prescott to pursue your dreams, while once again Julia is left behind."

"Well, jeez, not *permanently*. Besides, when was she left behind before?"

Abby softened. Dana actually watched her mother's face loosen. "I'm sorry. That's not what I meant. It's just that you — you're driven. You're on a true career path. That's a gift your father gave you."

"What are you saying? That Dad left Julia out? That he didn't give her a career path? Julia didn't want what Dad had, Mom, she only wanted what I had."

"My point exactly."

"This is so unfair!"

"Dana, calm down."

"You know, you're acting like nothing bad ever happens to me. All the bad things happen to Julia. And somehow they're my fault."

"Of course that's not what I mean. Although you have to admit that you *have* led a rather charmed life."

"*I* led a charmed life? Just me? I grew up in the same family Julia did and the same family Peter and Nell did. Do you think I'm responsible for Peter's Down syndrome, too?" Dana watched color rise in her mother's cheeks, but she couldn't stop the words that were forming in her brain. "Why did you *really* let me go back to New York, Mom? You let me go awfully easily. Was it because you thought Julia, Peter, and Nell needed you, but I didn't?"

"Dana! I let you go because that's what you wanted. Not that I ever had much say in your life anyway. You always do whatever you want to do. That's something else you —"

"Don't you dare say that's something else I got from Dad. And by the way, I work for the things I get. You're the one who said I was driven. Things aren't just handed to me."

Abby shook her head again. She turned angrily from Dana and glared out the window.

Dana watched her for a moment, then shoved her chair away from the table and said, "I don't know when Adele is going back to New York, but I'm leaving today."

"Don't you dare walk away, Dana. Don't you dare."

"Too late, Mom. You walked away from me a long time ago."

Epilogue

Dana leaned over the crib and reached for the baby's hand. She felt the fingers curl around her thumb, and she looked at the nails, impossibly tiny. She remembered that she'd been afraid to cut those nails when Francie was a newborn. She'd made Matthew do it for months until at last he'd said, "Dana, you have to learn to do this."

"Why?" she'd asked. Then she added, "I'll trade you poopy diapers for nail cutting."

Matthew had grinned. "Nope. You need to learn."

"Hi, sweet girl," Dana said now. "How long have you been awake?"

Francie smiled up at her mother. She waved her hands and kicked her feet.

"Oof," said Dana, picking her up. "You are the sweetest girl ever. And maybe the biggest."

Dana turned around to find Matthew smiling at her from the doorway of the nursery. He was so tall that his head nearly touched the top of the door frame. "I think Francie is going to be tall like you," said Dana. She set Francie on her hip and looped her arm through Matthew's, and they walked into the room that served as living room, dining room, and art studio. She studied the painting Matthew was working on. A commissioned painting. It was hard to believe that this time a year ago, they had still been students at Prescott — married students living in an apartment off campus, but students nevertheless — and already Matthew was getting commissions. The current piece showed the Swan Boats in the Public Garden in Boston. You had to squint to recognize the boats, but they were there, in Matthew's broad-stroked style.

Matthew walked across the room and stood before the painting. Nearby was a half-eaten bagel that he'd left on a footstool after breakfast. On the floor were a shirt and a single sock. On the back of an armchair was a page from the newspaper. All day long Matthew set things down and forgot about them. They became part of his landscape.

Dana didn't care. It was her landscape, too, and she liked it just the way it was. A room with a canvas leaning against the wall, a drawing table, an easel, a playpen, and a couch that had originally come from the street where someone had left it out for garbage pickup. All fine with her. Dana set

Francie in the playpen. "Okay, baby girl," she said. "Here's your bunny. Here's Bugs."

Dana settled herself at the drawing table. Matthew was holding a large brush coated in white paint, but not moving, lost in thought. Dana picked up a pencil and started sketching. She was employed part-time as a designer at a Boston publishing company, since they needed every cent they could earn. But her dream was still to illustrate books. That hadn't wavered.

"Are you going into work this afternoon?" asked Matthew, without turning around.

"Yup. But I'll be home by six." Dana hated leaving Francie, even though Matthew was a wonderful father. She'd had no idea how attached she would become to the baby — instantly attached — but the job at the publishing house had been too good to hope for. It had been offered to her a mere two months after she graduated from Prescott, and when she revealed that she was pregnant, her boss had arranged for her to work part-time after the baby was born. Dana knew she was very fortunate.

Dana and Matthew worked quietly. Francie crawled around the playpen. She gripped the bars, pulled herself to a standing position, and then fell over on purpose, laughing.

Matthew turned to look at her. "Remember when falling on your rump was the funniest thing in the world?" he asked.

"That's what attracted me to you."

This was true. Dana had noticed Matthew Goldberg on their very first day at Prescott. She had arrived on the campus tired and cranky, after a hot ride from Manhattan in a wreck of a car that Adele had borrowed from a friend, followed by a tearful good-bye with her aunt. She was standing glumly in her dorm room, having already decided that her roommate, Shelley, an adenoidal blonde with a custom-made tennis racket, was a dweeb.

"I claim the desk under the window," Shelley had just said.

"Fine," Dana had replied. She peered into the hallway. Suddenly the stairwell door had banged open and the handsomest guy she'd ever seen strode through it, carrying two very heavy-looking cartons.

He'd noticed Dana noticing him, had grinned and said, "Hey," in an overly casual way, and then tripped over a hockey stick, dropped the cartons, and fallen on his behind.

Dana couldn't help herself. She began to laugh. "I'm sorry!" she'd gasped. "I'm sorry." She hadn't laughed in weeks, but hadn't wanted to say so, hadn't wanted to tell a stranger about Julia or the awful, poisonous fight with her mother.

Matthew had started to laugh, too. He was still sprawled on the floor, the boxes beside him. After a few moments he said, "In case you couldn't tell, I'm not very coordinated."

That was the beginning of their friendship. Dana, who hadn't had a single serious boyfriend in high school, had fallen for Matthew in that instant. (Later, when she would tell the story to Francie, she would always say, "We *fell* for each other, pun intended.") Dana and Matthew had become friends on that first day of school, and not much later had become girlfriend and boyfriend, spending as much time together as possible. Less than two years later, during the summer after their sophomore year, they'd gotten married in a small ceremony at a chapel near campus.

Adele had been shocked when Dana announced the wedding. "But Prescott," she'd said. "Your career."

"Matthew and I are going to finish school," Dana assured her. "And I am definitely going to have a career. Don't worry. Anyway, I should think you'd be pleased that we're having a wedding and not just eloping or something."

Adele *had* been pleased about that, but couldn't help saying (more than once) that this wasn't quite what she'd had in mind for Dana. Still, she'd attended the wedding. So had

Julia. Abby had politely declined. And Papa Luther had become quietly furious.

"She's marrying a Jewish boy?" he'd said icily to Adele when she'd phoned him with the news.

Adele had sighed. "Yes, Matthew is Jewish."

Dana gathered that there hadn't been much more to the conversation. She'd understood that she would see little of Papa Luther from then on. Well, that was her family. She rarely saw her mother or Orrin either.

After the wedding, Dana and Matthew had moved into an apartment near the Prescott campus, worked hard for the next two years, graduated with honors (Dana was five months pregnant with Francie), and immediately moved to Boston, where they'd found their shabby, homey apartment. Matthew had been offered his first commission on the day Dana had been offered her design job. Two months later Francie had been born. After a tumultuous first few weeks, during which Matthew's mother and later Adele had arrived to help with the baby, Dana and Matthew had settled into a routine with Francie.

"It probably isn't a traditional routine," Dana had said one night as she and Matthew finally crawled into bed at three o'clock, each having finished an assignment just in the nick of time.

"But we aren't like most people."

Dana cherished her life with Matthew and Francie. It might not have been the life she'd envisioned for herself — not her life at twenty-two anyway — but, well, you couldn't plan everything.

"You know what?" she said to Matthew now. She lifted Francie out of the playpen and walked her around the room. "Tomorrow I'm going to talk to Roger and tell him I'm ready to come in full-time again. It will mean almost twice the money."

"But your work," said Matthew. "I mean, your own work, your art. When will you have time for that?"

Dana winced. "Later, I guess. But we need the money now. Francie will start preschool in a couple of years, and —"

The phone rang then. Matthew picked it up. "Hello?"

Dana carried Francie into her tiny room and changed her, dropping the soggy diaper into a pink plastic pail. Soon it would be time to wash yet another load of diapers, a chore she didn't mind as much as she'd thought she would. "There you are," she said to her daughter. "All nice and dry. All ready for —"

"Honey?" Matthew was standing in the doorway, looking stunned.

Dana felt a wave of fear wash over her. "Everything all right?" she asked.

"Yeah." Matthew ran his fingers through his curly hair. "I mean, yeah, it's *really* all right. I'm just sort of . . ." He shook his head. "That was Princeton. Princeton University. The head of the art department. I just got offered a teaching job."

"At *Princeton*?"

Matthew nodded.

"In Princeton, *New Jersey*?"

"Yes. This is amazing. I'd be teaching at one of the most prestigious universities in the country and I'd still have time to paint. They're offering a very nice salary. Money would be a lot less tight."

Matthew didn't say, "This is my dream job," but Dana knew that that's exactly what it was. Her husband's dream job.

And Dana didn't say, "What about *my* job?" since she wasn't sure she wanted her job. The money and the experience, yes. The job, not particularly. She shifted Francie to her other hip. What she did say was "We'd have to move to New Jersey. It's so far away."

"We'd be closer to Adele, though. And closer to my family.

You might even be able to get a job in New York and commute. If that's what you want."

Dana couldn't imagine leaving Francie with a babysitter while she went to New York and Matthew taught at the university.

"Honey?" said Matthew. Dana offered him a smile. "I know it's a big change, but just think about it, okay?"

She already knew what her answer would be.

She'd be leaving some things behind — some important things — but she'd always wanted to be an artist. Maybe the move to Princeton would allow her to seize, at last, what her father had hoped to give her.

"Yes," she said to Matthew. "Yes, let's go."

And just like that, she accepted Zander's gift.

About the Author

Ann M. Martin in the acclaimed and bestselling author of a number of novels and series, including *Belle Teal*, *A Corner of the Universe* (a Newbery Honor book), *A Dog's Life*, *Here Today*, *P.S. Longer Letter Later* (written with Paula Danziger), the Doll People series (written with Laura Godwin), the Family Tree series, the Main Street series, and the generation-defining series The Baby-sitters Club. She lives in New York.